THE BACKUP MEN

"Mr. Thomas [is] in his best form . . . awfully, awfully good."
—*The New Yorker*

"A high- and live-wire performance from start to finish."
—*Kirkus Reviews*

Also available in Perennial Library
by Ross Thomas:

THE COLD WAR SWAP
IF YOU CAN'T BE GOOD
THE MONEY HARVEST
THE PORKCHOPPERS
THE SEERSUCKER WHIPSAW
YELLOW-DOG CONTRACT

THE BACKUP MEN

ROSS THOMAS

Harper & Row, Publishers
New York, Cambridge, Philadelphia, San Francisco
London, Mexico City, São Paulo, Singapore, Sydney

A hardcover edition of this book was published in 1971 by William Morrow & Company, Inc. It is here reprinted by arrangement with William Morrow & Company, Inc.

 For information address William Morrow & Co., Inc., 105 Madison Avenue, New York, N.Y. 10016. Published simultaneously in Canada by Fitzhenry & Whiteside Limited, Toronto.

First PERENNIAL LIBRARY edition published in 1984. Reissued in 1986.

Library of Congress Cataloging-in-Publication Data

Thomas, Ross, 1926–
The backup men.

"Perennial Library."
Reprint. Originally published: New York : Morrow, 1971.
I. Title.
PS3570.H58B3 1986 813'.54 84-47674
ISBN 0-06-080833-0 (pbk.)

---

86 87 88 89 90 OPM 10 9 8 7 6 5 4 3 2 1

THE BACKUP MEN

Chapter 1

He didn't look old enough. Not old enough to order a martini at eleven forty-five in the morning, so when I got the small headshake from Joan, the cocktail waitress, I left the bar and a slightly hung-over reporter from *The Washington Post* and went to see whether the youthful morning drinker had anything to prove that he was at least twenty-one.

It was still too early for the luncheon trade and the reporter and I had been trading diet tips over a bottle of beer and reminiscing about an infantry replacement training center in north Texas where we'd both spent a few months a long time ago, hating every minute of it.

Even close up he didn't look old enough. I guessed him for nineteen, possibly twenty, but that may have been because of the pale blond, almost white hair that covered the tops of his ears and which he had carefully brushed and combed back into a revolutionary ducktail. The 1776 revolution, not the current one.

He didn't watch me approach. He didn't look up until I said, "Sorry to bother you, but have you got something that says you're over twenty-one? We'd like to keep the license."

He looked up then and when I saw his eyes, I felt that I'd make a mistake. When he smiled, I knew I had. Some people have dirty laughs, but he had a dirty smile and it had taken him a lot longer than twenty-one years to perfect it. He kept it in place while he reached into an inside pocket of his coat and brought out a thin black folding case and handed it to me. His eyes never left my face, eyes that were the palest of blue, almost the color of Arctic ice and nearly as compassionate.

He had handed me a Swiss passport and it claimed that his name was Walter Gothar and that he lived in Geneva and that he was thirty-two years old. I handed it back to him.

"Sorry, Mr. Gothar," I said.

"It happens frequently."

"The drink's on the house."

Gothar shook his head slightly. "I insist on paying." He had an accent, but it seemed to come and go depending on which word he used. I shrugged and gave him a nice enough smile and started to turn away when he said, "Where is Michael Padillo?" I turned back.

"In Chicago. On business."

"I regret that I have missed him."

"He'll be back tomorrow."

"I would like for you to give him a message."

"All right."

He paused for a long moment, as if troubled over the phrasing of the message, and it gave me the opportunity to admire his dark blue shirt and his white knit tie and the rich raw silk that had been used to run up his new spring suit. He wore a display handkerchief tucked away up his left sleeve and it matched the color of his shirt and I might have taken him for a bit of a fop were it not for those icy eyes and that dirty smile which came and went like a warning beacon above a smooth, stubborn chin that would seldom need a shave. His thin nose had character, too, but I wasn't sure what kind.

"You are the McCorkle?" he said and I said yes, I was the McCorkle. I turned and nodded at Joan and she quickly brought his martini over. After she had gone he removed two one-dollar bills from a thin brown wallet and smoothed them out on the table beside his drink, looking at it thoughtfully, but not touching it. He was still gazing at it when he said, "Tell Michael Padillo—" He stopped and looked up at me quickly, perhaps to make sure that I was really listening.

"Tell Padillo," he said slowly, spacing each word, "that we don't want to buy the farm."

"He'll be sorry to hear that," I said, just to be saying something.

He studied me some more, apparently not so much to see if I'd got the message, but whether I'd understood it. I thought I had, but I saw no reason to let Gothar know. I have cautious days like that.

"I must discuss my reasons with him personally."

"See him tomorrow."

"What time is best?"

"He usually gets here between ten thirty and eleven."

"You'll not forget the message?"

"No."

"And my name?"

"Walter Gothar." I'm good at remembering names and faces. It's about the only qualification needed to run a successful saloon.

Gothar rose from behind the banquette table in one smooth flowing motion. I saw that he was nearly as tall as I, something over six feet, and if he had kept his eyes closed and not smiled at anyone, he could have passed for some freshwater college's sophomore quarterback. He looked at me carefully once more, as if still debating whether I had enough sense to deliver his message, nodded in an abrupt, Teutonic way after apparently concluding that I did, turned and headed toward the entrance without touching his drink or saying good-bye or good day or even *auf Wiedersehen,* which probably was the language that he felt most comfortable in.

I picked up his drink and carried it back to the bar, trying to decide whether to drink it myself or sell it again. I decided to drink it myself and as I sat at the bar and sipped it and watched the first customers arrive I thought about the message that Gothar wanted me to give Padillo. It was World War II slang and I felt that he was a little young to be using it, but then I had thought that he was too young to be ordering a martini at eleven forty-five in the morning.

Those who had bought the farm during World War II had been those who'd died, of course, and if Gothar didn't want to buy it, that meant that he didn't want to die and he wanted Michael Padillo to know it.

I found that a little odd because at one time Padillo had sold the farm to a number of persons for one huggermugger government agency or other and there were those who considered him to be quite good at it. There were also a number of others who wished that he had bought himself one a long time ago.

Chapter 2

A few years back Michael Padillo and I had owned a saloon called Mac's Place in Bonn on the banks of the Rhine. It had been in Bad Godesberg really and there had been some trouble and the saloon had been dynamited and Padillo had disappeared for more than a year. I got married and opened another saloon in Washington a few blocks north of K Street and a little west of Connecticut Avenue. It's still called Mac's Place and nobody has dynamited it yet, although when Padillo reappeared there had been some more trouble with a local black gangster, a Federal narcotics agent, and the dying white prime minister of a South African country who had wanted Padillo to assassinate him, but it was nothing that couldn't be resolved without getting more than three or four persons killed. I scarcely even dream about it any longer.

Some say that Mac's Place is fading a little now, but I like to think that it has only mellowed. It's kept comfortably dim so that it can serve as a sanctuary for those who might like to have lunch or a drink with someone else's spouse. The service is quick, silent, and unobtrusive; the drinks are properly chilled and perhaps more than generous, and if you care for the latest gossip, you can sit at the bar and listen to Karl, the chief bartender, dissect character and reputation without fear or favor. The menu is admittedly limited and admittedly expensive, but if your taste runs to chicken and steak, it offers the best chicken and steak in town.

Padillo and I had been thinking about opening another place in one of four other towns and that was why he was in Chicago when Walter Gothar came calling. The cities we'd chosen, in addition to Chicago, were New York, Los Angeles, and San Francisco. I'd just spent a week checking out New York before concluding that it didn't really need another saloon. After Padillo got back from Chicago, I planned to look into San Francisco, because it was where I'd been born, and Padillo would check out Los Angeles because he had once lived there a long time ago.

The only reason that we even considered expanding is because our accountants had told us that we'd better do something with the profits or they'd go to help pay for an ABM system, or napalm or something equally useful. Another saloon made more sense than that, as almost anything would, so although neither of us were keen expansionists, it was still nice to travel around the country sampling what someday might become the competition.

When Padillo came in the next morning he looked relaxed, even carefree, so I decided that Chicago didn't need another saloon either. After we said hello he got himself a cup of coffee and brought it to the bar.

"How was it?" I said.

He shook his head. "It lacked the proper ambience." It was the same phrase that I'd used to report on New York. We both liked the word because one of the local restaurant columnists had once described Mac's Place as having a "definitely unusual ambience that bears investigation" and it had been days before Karl, our head bartender, would confess that he'd headed for the dictionary to make sure that the health authorities weren't going to close us down.

"When do you want to check out Los Angeles?" I said.

"Next month, I think. You still plan on San Francisco next week?"

I nodded. "Or the week after."

"What do you hear from Fredl?"

"The usual wish you were here stuff."

"Maybe you should have gone."

"I never liked Frankfurt that much," I said. My wife was Washington correspondent for one of the Frankfurt papers, the one that still uses columns to brood about whether England should be in the Common Market, and she had flown back to Germany for its annual editorial conference. Most of Washington's foreign correspondents called her either Fredl or Freddie, but back in Frankfurt she was Frau Doktor McCorkle, which must have created a fine guttural gurgle. Along with a good mind, my wife also had looks and style and wit and we seldom fought more than two or three times a year and I found myself missing her very much.

"Did I have any calls?" Padillo asked.

I took out several slips of paper and handed them over. They were telephone messages taken by either me or Herr Horst, our martinet of a maitre d' who got two percent of our net and who thought that Padillo should have been long married. The calls were mostly from young, breathless female voices who wanted to know when Mr. Padillo would be back in town and would I mind terribly asking him to call Margaret or Ruth or Helen as soon as he returned. "The one called Sadie sounded nice," I said. "Sort of old-fashioned."

Padillo riffled through the slips and nodded absently. "She plays French horn in the symphony," he said. "Anything else?"

"You got a message from one Walter Gothar."

Padilllo's smooth olive face assumed what I sometimes thought of as his Spanish look. His dark brown eyes narrowed and his mouth tightened into a thin line. I felt that it made him look something like a matador who's been slipped a bad bull. "A phone message?"

"No. He delivered it personally."

"Light hair, almost white? Looks as if he should register for the draft next week?"

"That's him."

"What'd he want?"

"He wanted me to tell you that he doesn't want to buy the farm."

Padillo put down his coffee cup and went around the bar and found the pinch bottle of Haig and poured himself a sizable drink. He looked at me and I shook my head no. Padillo sipped his Scotch and let his eyes wander around the empty room as if he were wondering how much it would all bring at a forced sale.

"Did Gothar say *he* doesn't want to buy it or *we* don't want to buy it?"

I tried to remember. "He said 'we'"

Some people never seem to frown and Padillo was one of them. But this time he did and it gave his face a strangely forbidding look. "He say anything else?"

"That he'd be by to see you today around this time. What is he, an old friend?"

Padillo shook his head. "His brother was. Older brother. We worked together a few times and we owed each other favors. I think I still owed him one when he got killed last year in Beirut. They said it was Beirut."

"His message seemed a little obvious, I thought."

Padillo sighed. He did that about as often as he frowned—once or twice a year. "When you're trying to stay alive you can't afford to be too subtle. But he did say 'we,' didn't he?"

"He said 'we.'"

"They work as a team."

"Doing what?"

Padillo lit a cigarette before answering. "Doing more or less what I used to do. It runs in the family. The Gothars have been at it since Napoleon's time. Karl Schulmeister brought them into the business around 1805. They're Swiss and they've always worked for the higher bidder. 'All brains and no heart,'" he said, phrasing the words the way people do when they're quoting someone else.

"Who said that about them?"

"General Savary said it about Schulmeister when he introduced him to Napoleon. But it also fits the Gothars—what's left of them. That's why I may seem a little surprised. They're not the kind to drop around asking for help."

"Who's the other half of the team?" I said.

"Gothar's twin."

I pointed at the Haig. "I think I will join you after all. A matched set of Gothars seems a little rich."

"They're not really a matched set," Padillo said, pouring my drink.

"You mean they're not identical twins?"

"They're identical twins all right, but you won't have any trouble telling them apart."

"Why?"

"Because Walter Gothar's twin is called Wanda."

Chapter 3

They came in together about half an hour later, blinking at our perpetual twilight and looking as much alike as two persons can and still be different sexes—something like two nickel-plated ball bearings that are labeled him and her.

Although she had the same chilly eyes, Wanda Gothar's smile failed to match her brother's in nastiness, but then I only saw her smile twice and I don't think she really tried either time.

Padillo swung around on his bar stool and watched them approach. He didn't smile either. Instead, he kept his eyes on them much as a mongoose would keep its eyes on twin cobras. I began to wonder whether I should summon Herr Horst and tell him to lock up the good silver.

When he was only a few feet away, Walter Gothar stopped and performed one of his abrupt Teutonic nods that would have produced a bad case of whiplash in any normal person's neck. Then he said, "Padillo."

"How are you, Walter?" Padillo said, and then added indifferently, "You, too, Wanda."

She neither smiled nor nodded at Padillo. Instead, she seemed to look right through him with a gaze that denied his existence. She was shorter than her brother by five or six inches, but still tall for a woman, and where his jaw appeared stubborn, hers seemed only determined, and where his mouth was a taut line of stern discipline, hers had been expertly touched up into something that seemed fuller and softer, but still under rigid control.

You wouldn't want to call Walter Gothar pretty boy, his eyes wouldn't let you do that, but you could get by with exquisite and he probably wouldn't have minded at all. Lovely would have done for his sister, although she seemed indifferent to what anyone called her, unless all that careful casualness of walk and stance and movement was a deliberate pose, which it may well have been.

"You received my message," Gothar said, flicking his gaze from Padillo to me as though to indicate that he was aware of my existence, but didn't feel that it required any formal acknowledgment.

"I got it," Padillo said and then introduced me to Wanda Gothar with "Miss Gothar, Mr. McCorkle, my partner."

She nodded in my general direction, but still said nothing.

"We wish to discuss it with you," Gothar said. "Privately."

Padillo shook his head. "You know better than that, Walter. I wouldn't discuss the price of a drink with you unless I had a witness."

"It is confidential matter," Gothar said.

"McCorkle is a confidential person."

Gothar looked at his sister and once more she nodded, if moving your chin up and down a bare quarter of an inch can be called a nod. Gothar glanced around the still empty bar and made a brief, disdainful gesture with his right hand. "Isn't there some other place where we could talk?"

"We have an office," Padillo said. "Will that do?"

Gothar said that it would and they followed Padillo through the dining area and I tagged along behind, feeling unwanted, if not unneeded, and only mildly interested in what Walter Gothar's confidential matter was all about. I was far more interested in his sister's long, slender legs that flashed beneath the pale gray skirt of her knit suit that did nothing to conceal her other charms, which were considerable. I'm not too good at assessing women's clothes, but I would have put a three-hundred-dollar price tag on Wanda Gothar's knit suit and bet another hundred that I wasn't more than ten dollars off. Walter Gothar had on a different suit from yesterday, a double-breasted gray one with lots of buttons, but I couldn't get interested in what it had cost.

Our office wasn't much except for the antique partners' desk that Fredl had given us last Christmas and which we used sparingly because we were afraid that one of us would absentmindedly set a wet glass on its highly polished oak surface. There was the desk and a comfortable enough couch, two straight-backed chairs, three green filing cabinets, two black phones, a gaudy calendar, and a window with a view of the alley.

Padillo and I sat at the desk. Walter Gothar chose the couch and his sister sat in one of the two chairs, her knees together and her ankles crossed.

Padillo leaned back in his chair, almost put his feet on the desk, but caught himself in time, and said, "What are you working on, Walter?"

"A protection assignment."

"Anybody I know?"

"Do you mean our client?"

"No."

"Then you must mean our antagonist?"

"That's a pretty way to say it."

"It's Kragstein."

Padillo was silent as if skimming a mental file on Kragstein. After a moment or two he said, "He's not that good anymore."

"Gitner is with him."

Padillo didn't need to examine his file on Gitner. He said, "Then you have got trouble."

"That is why we need a—uh—backup man," Gothar said and looked a trifle proud of his adroit use of the colloquialism.

Padillo shook his head. Firmly. "I'm out of it," he said. "I have been for a couple of years."

Wanda Gothar looked at him, not through him for the first time, and smiled before she spoke, but the chill in her tone canceled any meaning the smile may have had. "You'll never be out of it, Michael. I told you that seven years ago in Bucharest."

"You told me a lot of things in Bucharest, Wanda, but none of them was true."

"And for how long have you been an authority on truth?"

"I'm not," he said, "but I'm damned good when it comes to lies."

Walter Gothar quickly interrupted what could have developed into a nasty quarrel between old rivals or old lovers. Or both. I was never really sure. "You must at least consider it."

"No," Padillo said.

"I told you he wouldn't," Wanda said to her brother.

Walter Gothar gave her q quick, annoyed glance before asking Padillo, "Is it Gitner that disturbs you?"

"Amos Gitner should disturb anyone who's not a

fool," Padillo said, "but he doesn't disturb me because I won't be messing around with him."

"Could it be Kragstein who—"

"Franz Kragstein's getting old," Padillo interrupted. "He can't move like he once did, but there's nothing wrong with his brain and if he's got Gitner to run the errands, then it doesn't matter whether he can move or not. I saw Gitner in action once and he's faster and younger than any of us."

If the man called Amos Gitner had reflexes which made him faster than Padillo, then he was indeed in superb condition. Although the pronounced frosting of gray in my partner's dark hair wasn't all that premature, he had one of those rare natural athlete's bodies that seem to keep themselves in perfect shape without any conscious effort on the part of their occupants. He ate what he wanted, smoked as much as I, drank nearly as much, and could run the hundred in ten seconds flat wearing street clothes and afterwards be breathing no more heavily than I—should I ever have occasion to jog around the block, which I won't. He also spoke six or seven languages perfectly, knew all there was to know about guns and knives, was a bit of a ladies' man, if not an out-and-out rake, and there were some days that I was mildly bitter about it all.

"We do not need him," Wanda Gothar said and rose.

"I don't think you do either," Padillo said. "What's the assignment?"

"Interested?" she asked.

"Curious."

"Sit down, Wanda," Walter said. She hesitated briefly and then resumed her seat in the chair.

Walter Gothar frowned, as if thinking deeply, and then said, "Our problem is that our client is traveling incognito. Otherwise, we could draw on your Secret Service."

"You could anyway, if he's the friendly type," Padillo said.

Gothar shook his head. "He refuses to hear of it. He insists that there be no official recognition of his visit, formal or informal."

"Does he know about Kragstein and Gitner?"

"Yes."

"Then he's a fool."

"In some ways."

Padillo stood up. "Well, I'm sorry I can't help."

"The money will be excellent," Gothar said.

Padillo shook his head. "I've got enough."

"No one has enough," Wanda said.

"It depends on what you think you can buy with it."

"Your philosophy was always on the cheap side, Padillo."

"I seem to recall when you thought it was the most valuable kind around."

"That was before I knew what a—"

"Please!" Gothar said, but it was more of a demand than a request. His sister shifted her gaze from Padillo and let it settle on the calendar. Padillo smiled faintly. Gothar rose, reaching into his inside pocket. He brought out an envelope and extended it toward Padillo. "It is from Paul to you," he said. "I have no choice."

Padillo hesitated before accepting the envelope. Then he took it, examined the blue wax seal on its flap, ripped it open, and swiftly read it. "I recognize his handwriting," Padillo said, handing the letter to me. "Do you know what it says?"

"We have no idea," Gothar said. "He told us that we might need it some day."

"It's from their brother," Padillo explained to me. "He's dead now. He died last year in Beirut, wasn't it?"

Gothar nodded. "In Beirut."

The undated letter was written with black ink in a neat European scrawl that was all sharp, tight angles and unfinished descenders. It was in English and it read, "My dear Padillo, Some day the twins will find themselves with one which they may have the sense to realize that they cannot handle alone. We have exchanged favors many times and I am no longer sure whether I owe you or you owe me, but I hope that it does not matter. Please do what you can for them, if you can. I shall be, let us say, eternally grateful. Sincerely, Paul Gothar."

"He wrote a nice hand," I said, handing the note back. Padillo nodded and passed the note to Gothar who read it and gave it to his sister. While she was reading it, Gothar said, "Well?"

Padillo shook his head. "I'm not that sentimental, Walter. Maybe if your brother hadn't been, he'd still be alive."

"We don't need him, Walter," Wanda Gothar said.

The tall man with the too young face jerked his head in another of his neck-cricking nods and moved to the door, holding it open for his sister. She swept through it with what I thought was a fair amount of disdain. Gothar paused to look at Padillo thoughtfully. "We won't beg," he said, "but should you change your mind, one of us will be at the Hay-Adams."

"I won't change my mind," Padillo said. "Besides, I think you're badmouthing yourselves. You don't really need me."

"That is something that the next few days will determine," Gothar said, turning to leave.

"Good luck," Padillo said.

Gothar paused once more to give Padillo a cold stare. "In our business, Padillo, luck plays a very small role," he said and then he was gone.

"You want a drink?" I said, picking up the phone.

"A martini."

I dialed a single number and ordered. "Why didn't you lend a hand?" I said. "It was nice note."

Padillo smiled slightly. "There was only one thing wrong with it," he said.

"What?"

"Paul Gothar couldn't read or write English."

Chapter 4

I may be one of the last persons in Washington to walk its streets late at night. I do so because I like to and because of a perverse conviction that the city's sidewalks were built to be used twenty-four hours a day, just as they are used in such cities as London and Paris and Rome.

I've had some trouble a couple of times, but that's largely my lookout. Once it was a trio of young hoods who thought a fight might be fun and then whimpered when they found that it wasn't. The other time was when two muggers decided that they had need of my watch and wallet, but crawled off down an alley without them. I wrote both incidents off as my contribution to law and order. In New York, of course, I take cabs. I'm not a complete fool.

It was usually a little after midnight when I got home, which was on the eighth floor of an apartment building located just south of Dupont Circle. If the neighborhood wasn't as fashionable as Georgetown, it had more flavor, and that's what city living supposedly is all about. Within a one-block radius, I needed no more than three minutes to contract for either a bag of heroin or an angel food cake and that must have been what the apartment's management meant when it advertised the place as being convenient to fine shopping.

I walked home later than usual the Tuesday

night that the Gothar twins called on Padillo. It had been one of those relatively rare spring days in Washington when even the three-packs-a-day boys can smell the magnolias. The dinner trade had been particularly good, the chef had been sober, the annual income tax nick promised to be less traumatic than usual, and nothing but mild guilt would prevent me from sleeping till noon.

The editors at *House Beautiful* would have blanched at our two-bedroom apartment because it was furnished with the disparate possessions of two persons who've married a little late in life and whose tastes have already been shaped and molded into what some might regard as prejudice. We usually agreed on paintings, but when it came to furniture Fredl favored what I regarded as unhappy Hepplewhite while she more than once had accused me of trying to turn the place into the Senior Members' Room at the Racquet Club. There had been a series of painfully negotiated compromises, but I'd drawn the line at The Chair.

I had won it with three of a kind in college and it had crossed the Atlantic twice and if its leather was a bit worn and the springs sagged a little, it was still The Chair and I'd read some fine books in it and used it to doze away some dull afternoons and even made some big plans in it, and if they hadn't quite materialized, it wasn't The Chair's fault.

When I arrived home that night and opened the door and switched on the light, I knew what Papa Bear must have felt like because someone had been sitting in my chair—was still sitting in it, sprawled in it really, his head back, his hands in his lap, and his feet stuck straight out in front of him. His eyes were open and so was his mouth and his tongue, dark and swollen, bulged out of it. Two white plastic bicycle handlebar grips lay on his chest on top of a broad green and gray foulard tie. The grips were attached to the piano wire that had been used to choke the life out of Walter Gothar.

He may have put up some kind of a struggle, but there was no sign of it. No lamps were knocked over. The ashtrays, full as usual, were neatly in place. So perhaps all he had done was to claw at the wire that bit into his neck while he drummed his heels on the carpet. It was a rotten way to die because it took so long—possibly two minutes depending on the skill and the strength of the garroter.

I crossed the room and picked up the phone and dialed 444-1111 and when the man's voice said, "Police emergency," I gave him my name and address, told him that a man had been killed in my apartment, and then hung up. I dialed another number and when Padillo answered, I said, "Your friend Walter Gothar."

"What about him?"

"He's dead."

"Where?"

"In my chair. Somebody garroted him. Piano wire and plastic handlebar grip. I think it's piano wire."

"Cops on the way?"

"I just called them."

"I'll be there in five minutes."

"If they get here first, is there anything you want me not to tell them?"

Padillo was silent for a moment until he said, "No. Nothing."

"Then I might try the truth."

"They might even believe you," he said and hung up. I understand that you're not supposed to touch anything, but I had a small bar in one corner so I went over and poured myself a Scotch, reasoning that the killer might not have liked the brand, or perhaps hadn't wanted to hang around leaving fingerprints all over a glass while he toasted his handiwork.

Holding the drink, I stood there in the center of the living room and stared at the dead body of Walter Gothar and wondered why he had wanted to see me, and how he'd got into my apartment, and whether he had known the person who had produced the wire and looped it around his neck, pulling it tight from behind until the spinal cord went or until lack of oxygen destroyed the brain. Either way, Walter Gothar was thoroughly dead so I stood there and wondered what that was like until Padillo knocked at the door.

He came in and crossed over to Gothar's body and quickly went through the pockets. He took nothing and replaced everything carefully, using his coat sleeve to wipe away or smear his fingerprints. When he was through he straightened and stared down at the dead man.

"Not pretty anymore, is he?"

"Not very," I said. "Did you call his sister?"

Padillo shook his head and moved over to the bar. "I'll let the cops do that."

"Find anything in his pockets?"

"He has an interesting set of keys."

After Padillo poured his own drink we continued to stand in the center of the living room, like two persons who don't know anybody else at a chairless cocktail party. We stood there, not saying much, until the police arrived. After that we both found plenty to talk about.

Counting manslaughters, there had been 327 murders in the Washington area during the past year and the two homicide squad cops who'd drawn the Gothar death looked as if they had been stuck with at least half of them. The two cops were black and white and they didn't seem to care much for each other and not at all for Padillo and me.

The white cop was a detective sergeant, a tall, sour man of about thirty-three or -four with bleached blue eyes that somehow went with the whine in his West Virginia accent. He introduced himself as Sergeant Lester Vernon and I decided that he probably was a sixth- or seventh-generation American WASP who thought that poking around dead bodies was better than mining coal. Maybe it was.

The black cop was Lieutenant Frank Schoolcraft. He was a few years older than Vernon and he had a big wide nose and a big wide mouth and looked as if he would speak with a mushy accent and use *man* every other word, but he didn't. Instead, he talked out of the left side of his mouth because something had happened to the muscles on the right side and he seemed a little self-conscious about it. If he had any accent at all, it was East Coast Bitter.

"So when you found him you called us and then you called your partner here?" Schoolcraft said, nodding his long head at Padillo.

"That's right," I said.

"Why'd you call him?" Vernon said. "Whyn't you call a lawyer?"

"Because I'm not going to need a lawyer," I said.

"Huh," Vernon said and went over to look at the dead body some more.

The two of them had been questioning Padillo and me for twenty minutes and during that time a half dozen uniformed cops had flowed in and out of the apartment, doing nothing useful that I could see. The technical crew was still at work, but I didn't pay much attention to them. After thirty minutes or so they wheeled the body of Walter Gothar out of my apartment and I was glad to see him go.

Sergeant Vernon joined us again. "Never seen that before," he said.

"What?" Schoolcraft said.

"Those plastic handlebar grips. They had lead pipe inside of them and the pipe had little holes bored in it and the wire went in and out of those holes so it wouldn't slip." There was nothing but admiration in Vernon's voice.

"Seems funny to me," Schoolcraft said.

"What seems funny?" Vernon said.

"That a man would go to all that trouble to fix up something like that and then leave it behind. Anybody who'd go to all that trouble was planning on using that thing more than once. What do you think, Mr. Padillo?"

"I don't," Padillo said.

"And you don't know where his sister might be either?"

"Gothar told me the Hay-Adams."

"We tried that again and she's still not there."

Padillo looked at his watch. "It's only one-fifteen," he said. "Maybe she's out on the town."

Padillo's observation was about as pertinent and useful as the rest of the information that he had given the police about Walter and Wanda Gothar. Yes, he had known Walter Gothar and his sister for some time, nearly fifteen years, but no, he didn't know exactly why they were in Washington, although they had mentioned they were here on business, but he wasn't sure of its exact nature because they hadn't told him, and no, he didn't think he knew who might have wanted Walter dead.

"And they just dropped by to see you socially, is that it?" Schoolcraft said.

"I didn't say that," Padillo said.

"What was the reason?"

"They wanted to know if I would be interested in one of their ventures."

"Business ventures?"

"It could be called that, I suppose."

"What kind of business?"

"The confidential kind."

"So you don't know what it was?"

"No."

"What kind of business were the Gothars in as a rule?"

"I'm not sure that there were any rules in their business."

"Is that supposed to be a smartassed answer?"

"Just informative."

Schoolcraft shook his head. "You're about as informative as a fireplug. What kind of business?"

"Security," Padillo said.

"That doesn't tell me anything either."

"Think about it," Padillo said, turned, and headed for the bar.

"Your partner's not much help, is he?" Vernon said, giving me a nice, friendly smile.

"He's just withdrawn," I said.

"What about you?"

"I'm more outward going. You know, friendly."

"Is that why Gothar was in your apartment, because he liked the friendly types?"

"He was kind of cute, wasn't he?" I said and watched to see what effect the remark would have on Vernon. He didn't blush, but he couldn't prevent the look of uncomfortable disapproval from sliding across his face.

"Jesus, you don't look like a—"

"He's needling you, Sergeant," Schoolcraft said. "He's a smartass just like his partner."

Padillo came back from the bar, carrying two drinks. He handed one of them to me. That was thoughtful. I smiled at Vernon and took a swallow.

"Why was Gothar in your apartment, McCorkle?" Schoolcraft said, his voice a tired rasp.

I sighed and shook my head, keeping the impatience out of most of what I said. "I don't know why he was in my apartment. I don't know how he got in. He was here when I arrived and he was as dead then as he was when they wheeled him out of here ten minutes ago. And that makes him your responsibility, not mine, so why don't you go look for who killed him someplace else now that you've peeked under my bed and into all the closets."

I raised the glass for another swallow, but Lieutenant Schoolcraft knocked it out of my hand. The glass bounced on the carpet and the drink made a small puddle for a moment before the woolen fibers soaked it up.

"You should take something for that temper, Lieutenant," I said, bending down for the glass. When I straightened up, Schoolcraft was massaging his right hand. He couldn't possibly have hurt it.

"Eighteen hours straight today," he said. "Twenty yesterday, nineteen and a half the day before." He looked up from his hand. "I had no call to do that. Sorry."

"Forget it," I said and noticed that Sergeant Vernon seemed irritated by my magnanimity.

"Let's take them both down," Vernon said.

"Sure," Schoolcraft said, nodding wearily as he moved toward the door. "That would do everybody a lot of good, wouldn't it?"

"It might learn them not to be so goddamned lippy."

Schoolcraft turned at the door and leaned against it. He seemed to be a man who rested whenever he could. Only his eyes moved, racing across my face and then Padillo's circling the room quickly and finally lighting for a brief moment on Sergeant Vernon's face before again taking up their restless journey.

"A trip downtown wouldn't teach these two anything, Sergeant," he said. "You want to know why?"

"Why?" Lester said.

"Because you can't teach anything to guys who know it all—and you know it all, don't you, Padillo?"

"Not all of it," Padillo said. "For instance, I don't know what goes on inside a cop's head."

Schoolcraft stopped his eyes on Padillo's face. It was a hard, almost brutal stare. "You think it's different from what goes on inside your head?"

"It has to be."

"Why?"

"Because," Padillo said, "I could never be a cop."

Chapter 5

When the two homicide detectives had gone after making sure that we'd be down at police headquarters to make a full statement by 2 P.M., which was as soon as Lieutenant Schoolcraft would be out of court, I went into the kitchen and put on some water for coffee. It helps me to sleep for some inexplicable reason. Just as the water was beginning to boil there was a knock at the door. After I opened it I wished that I hadn't.

I knew the man who stood there with the oyster-white raincoat buttoned up to his neck and the lilac pajama bottoms that poked out from beneath his uncuffed gray flannels. He had been bad news when I'd first met him several years ago in Bonn and he was probably bad news now and I saw no reason to pretend that I was glad to see him at two o'clock in the morning.

"It couldn't wait, huh?" I said.

Stan Burmser shook his head and frowned so that three vertical creases appeared in his forehead, sure sign that he was thinking. Or trying to.

"He's here, isn't he?"

"He's helping me put up some marmalade."

Burmser shook his head again, a little sadly, I thought. "Still the sick comic," he said. "I thought you might've gone into therapy by now."

I turned my head. "You need anything from the Harvard man?" I called to Padillo.

He appeared in the foyer and looked at Burmser. He took his time. "I think your pajamas are ducky," Padillo said.

"So does my wife."

"What have you got, a police teletype in your bedroom?"

"Just a phone."

Padillo shrugged and turned back toward the living room. "Let's get it over with," he said.

I motioned Burmser to my chair where they had found Walter Gothar dead and he lowered himself into it without any obvious discomfort. I toyed with the idea of telling him who had sat in it last, but decided not to. It probably wouldn't have bothered him; he might even have enjoyed it.

"What happened to Gothar?" Burmser asked Padillo.

"He got himself killed."

"Why here?"

"Maybe because of its convenient in-town location."

"We knew the twins were around. We know that they saw you. We want to know why."

"Ask Wanda."

"I don't want to have to put somebody on you, Padillo."

"I won't mind as long as he's got a cheery manner and doesn't try to run up a tab."

I rose. "You want some coffee?" I said to Burmser.

He looked at his watch. "It's past two o'clock."

"I didn't ask what time it was."

"No, thanks,"

I made two cups of instant coffee and brought them into the living room, handing one to Padillo who claimed that it never kept him awake either. Burmser watched us drink it, not trying to hide his disapproval.

"I realize that you're no longer with us, Padillo."

"I never was. I was an indentured servant, if anything."

"You got paid."

"Not enough. Nobody's ever paid enough for what you wanted."

"You could have said no."

"I can now; I couldn't then. I tried, remember? How many times did I try to say no, a dozen? And each time until the last one you found a new pressure point that made me say yes and pack my bag and catch the next plane heading east for some place like Breslau with the odds eight to five and rising that I wouldn't make it back."

"Well, you're out of it for good now."

"Sure."

"All I'm after is information."

"I run a saloon, not an inquiry service."

"The twins wanted something. What?"

Padillo rose, moved over to the window, pulled back the curtain slightly, and looked out. If he'd craned his neck a little, he could have seen the Washington Monument and beyond that, the Potomac. I don't think he saw anything.

"A backup man," he said after several moments.

"You?"

"Me."

"Why you? I don't mean that like it sounds."

"They thought I owed their brother something."

"Paul? He's dead."

Padillo turned from the window. Burmser watched him carefully, as if waiting for him to go on with a particularly fascinating tale. When Padillo said nothing, but instead wandered over to look at a fairly good Irish seascape, Burmser cleared his throat.

"What were they on?" he said, trying to make his question casual, and almost bringing it off.

"A protection job."

"Who?"

"They didn't say. Somebody important enough to be able to afford them."

"Why a backup man?"

Padillo turned from his inspection of the painting and smiled at Burmser for the first time. "Franz Kragstein," he said, as if he enjoyed saying the name. "You remember Franz."

Burmser seemed to relax. He sank back into the chair that Walter Gothar had been strangled in and crossed his legs and produced a cigarette and lit it with a chrome lighter. Padillo wandered over to another painting, a turn-of-the-century portrait that I'd paid too little for a long time ago.

"Kragstein shouldn't have bothered them much," Burmser said.

Padillo cocked his head, as if trying to make up his mind about the portrait. "This guy really had it. Didn't he?" he said and, not expecting an answer, told Burmser, "It wasn't Kragstein who bothered them. It was his new partner. Or maybe associate."

"Who?"

"Amos Gitner," Padillo said and turned to watch the show.

It was worth it. Burmser let his jaw drop and then stubbed out his cigarette as if he were giving them up forever. When he was through with that the three vertical furrows reappeared in his forehead, deeper than before. I remembered them as a sign that he was now not only thinking, but also deeply worried. He rose hurriedly. "Can I use your phone?"

"You may," I said, doing my snide bit to keep the language pure.

He turned to Padillo once more. "Is he in the country?"

"Amos? I don't know."

"Come on, Padillo, who's the twins' client?"

"I guess he'd be Wanda's now, but I still don't know who he is. I don't know anything about him at all except that he's either here or coming here incognito and Amos Gitner doesn't bother him, which doesn't make him too smart in my book."

"Mine either," Burmser said and hurried over to the phone. He picked it up and then put it back down, turning to me. "Do you have another one?"

"In the bedroom. Down the hall and to the left."

When Burmser came back a few minutes later, his gray hair was rumpled as if he'd been running a hand through it out of nervousness or frustration or both. By then he must have been the civilian equivalent of a two-star general in that weird outfit he worked for, the one that had kept sending Padillo on those hurry-up trips when he should have been helping me inventory the booze. Padillo was out of it now, just as he said. He had got out the hard way, getting himself shot in the process, and I was more than curious to see whether he could stay out.

Burmser ran his hand over his hair again, bearing down hard as if trying to press away his look of mild embarrassment.

"*He* wants to talk to you," Burmser said to Padillo.

"Who?"

"Maybe it's the President," I said.

"I didn't vote for him."

"Maybe that's what he wants to talk to you about."

"For Christ's sake, Padillo, he's waiting."

Padillo crossed to the living room phone and after he picked it up and said hello he listened for what seemed to be a long time, but which couldn't have been more than three minutes. I guessed that he was listening to the man who ran Burmser's outfit, a publicity-shy multimillionaire who had once been a Rhodes scholar and who had gone into the business during World War II and had never done anything else. I assumed that he liked it.

Finally Padillo said, "I'll want that in writing on White House stationery." He listened for another fifteen or twenty seconds before he said, "You can call it blackmail; I'll call it insurance. If you think the price is too high, forget it." Impatience spread across his face as he listened a while longer before he said, "I don't work that way. When it's done it'll be done and you can hold all the postmortems you want, but don't count on me to be there . . . All right . . . Yes, I understand . . . Here he is." He held out the phone to Burmser who took it, said hello, listened fifteen seconds, said, "Yes, sir," but didn't get a chance to say good-bye because the connection was broken with a click that was audible across the room.

Burmser turned to look at Padillo. "He says you're solo."

"That's right."

"What about him?" Burmser said, nodding in my

direction as if I were some unwelcome intruder who'd bumbled his way into the conversation. Maybe I was.

Padillo looked at me thoughtfully. "We could tie him up and gag him and hide him in the closet."

"Aw, Christ," Burmser said, turning toward the door, "I don't know why I talk to either of you." He paused at the door with his hand on its knob. "You know where to reach me, Padillo."

"Don't sit by the phone."

"Amos Gitner," Burmser said and then repeated the name as if it cheered him considerably. "You still think you're all that good?"

"I guess I'll just have to find that out, won't I?" Padillo said.

"Yes," Burmser said, smiling broadly this time. "I guess we all will."

He opened the door and was halfway through it when I called to him. "You forgot something."

He stopped and turned. "What?"

"You forgot to hang up the phone in the bedroom."

Chapter 6

"What's do they want you to do?" I said after Burmser slammed the door hard enough to wake three floors of neighbors.

"Keep Wanda Gothar's client alive."

"Do they know who he is?"

"Burmser's boss does. Or says he does."

"Is he important?"

Padillo sank back in the sofa and stretched out his legs, staring at the ceiling. "He could be the richest kid in the world. If he lives long enough."

"He's important all right."

"You've heard about what's been going on in what they now call Llaquah?"

I thought a moment before answering. "It's way down the Persian Gulf, about the size of Delaware. It's also an absolute monarchy with a new oil strike that supposedly makes Kuwait look like a dry hole."

"Well, the kid's going to be the king of Llaquah as soon as his brother gets through dying."

"The playboy brother," I said. "I read somewhere that he had an accident last month. In France, I think."

Padillo nodded, still staring at the ceiling. "He flipped his Maserati while doing one-hundred-and-thirty. He was badly burned and his chest was crushed and I don't know what they're keeping him alive with. Prayer probably. But he's now something of a medical curiosity because by rights he should have been dead weeks ago."

"When does the wicked uncle come in?" I said.

"What wicked uncle?"

"The one who filed the tie rods on the Maserati and now is just waiting to do in the younger brother."

Padillo stared at me. "I thought you'd sworn off those late movies."

"I sneak one now and again."

"Well, there's no wicked uncle, but there are a couple of oil companies."

"That's almost as good," I said. "Two giant industrial combines locked in a death struggle over a tiny corner of the world which contains the richest oil reserves known to—"

"No death struggle," Padillo said. "They're in cahoots—a cooperative venture, I think it's called."

"But nothing so grand as a cartel?"

"No."

"What's the kid's name?"

"Peter Paul Kassim."

"Peter Paul?"

Padillo nodded and stretched. He yawned, too. I caught it and yawned back. "That seems to be one of his problems," he said after we were through yawning at each other. "At sixteen he underwent a religious experience and rejected his Muslim faith, converted to Catholicism, and entered a French monastery where he's been ever since."

"I take it that the folks back home didn't much care for that."

"Not much."

"Why is he in the States? His brother's not dead yet."

"They never got along and when the brother dies and Peter Paul becomes king, the oil companies are going to need his signature on the documents that will complete their deal. The older brother was to have signed them here, but he flipped his car before he could make the trip."

"How old is Peter Paul?"

"Twenty-one."

"Who wants him dead?"

Padillo yawned again. "Not the oil companies."

"No."

"There's no wicked uncle."

"Pity."

"So that's what I'm supposed to do. Keep Peter Paul alive and at the same time find out who wants him dead."

"And you said yes."

"No. I only said that I'd try to keep him alive."

"For how long?"

"Until his brother dies and he automatically becomes king and signs the documents."

"What about afterwards?"

"Right now Peter Paul hasn't got a dime. The Gothar twins must have taken him on spec—a contingency basis. When he signs those oil company contracts, or whatever they are, he gets five million dollars for his personal use. He can hire his own army then."

"Why don't the oil companies move in, if they want him to stay alive?"

"They don't want to get caught in a crossfire. If something happens to Peter Paul, they're fully prepared to do business with his successor—whoever he may be."

"What about the folks back home?"

"They won't lift a finger because of his infidel dog religion. They'd probably be just as happy if he got himself killed."

"So that leaves you and Wanda Gothar. I'd think that Peter Paul would welcome the Secret Service after what happened to Walter."

Padillo shrugged and rose. "Maybe he's just trying to find out how it feels to have royal prerogatives."

"Or he's stupid."

"There's always that possibility."

"Why?" I said.

"You mean why did I take it?"

"That's right."

Padillo moved to the door before answering. "I want that letter."

"On White House stationery."

Padillo nodded. "On White House stationery."

I shook my head. "You don't need it anymore. Five years ago maybe, but not now. You have more than enough to blackmail them with if you really wanted to say no."

Padillo smiled, but he wasn't looking at me. He was looking at the chair—at the last chair that Walter Gothar ever sat in. "Maybe I've gone in for coercion," he said.

"No. You're not much good at that either. And they won't write anything that you could really use."

"I thought there might be a line or two in it thanking me for doing another swell job for God and country."

"It was Walter Gothar getting himself killed here in my apartment, wasn't it?"

Padillo shrugged and put his hand on the door

knob. "There was that," he said, "and something else."

"What?"

"Maybe I do owe the twins' older brother a favor."

"He's dead and you're not that sentimental."

"That's right," Padillo said. "I'm not, am I?"

Padillo showed me the letter when it arrived by special White House messenger the next afternoon. It thanked him for his services, but after that it got a little vague. In fact, it was as fine a piece of obfuscated prose as I'd ever read.

Padillo held it up to the light to admire the watermark. "Did you ever hear of the guy who signed it?"

"No."

"I think he's in charge of the second-floor washrooms."

"It's on White House stationery though. That's what you asked for."

"So I did."

"What are you going to do with it?"

Padillo refolded the letter and put it back in its envelope. "Do you still have your safe-deposit box?"

I nodded. Padillo handed me the letter. "Put it in there for me, will you?"

"Sure," I said. "It's a pretty valuable document, all right."

"What do you keep in that box?"

"My own valuables."

"Such as?"

"Well, there's my eighteen-ninety-eight Indian head penny."

"My."

"And there's the original manuscript of my prize-winning essay entitled, 'What America Means to Me,' written at age nine."

"Priceless."

"There's also my Army discharge and twenty shares of Idaho Power and Light, and one thousand dollars case money in small bills. And should something happen to Fredl, she gave me the only copy in existence of her secret recipe for Denver chili."

"That letter's going to feel right at home," Padillo said.

"Of course, if he's not reelected, the letter won't be worth much."

"I've already got that figured out."

"How?"

"Next time he runs, I plan to vote for him."

We dropped the White House letter off at my bank on our way down to police headquarters where we spent an hour making statements for Lieutenant Schoolcraft. Sergeant Vernon wasn't around, nor was I interested enough to ask whether it was his day off.

Padillo and I dictated our separate statements into a tape recorder and while we waited for them to be transcribed we sat in a small office on the third floor of Metropolitan Police Headquarters on Indiana Avenue, Northwest. Time slows down once you start dealing with the police. It slows down even further if they manage to put you someplace where they can turn a key in a lock. The office that we waited in contained nothing to hurry time up. It contained three desks, three telephones, a couple of aging manual typewriters, some chairs, and Lieutenant Schoolcraft.

He sat behind one of the desks. Padillo and I sat in a couple of chairs that didn't match each other or any of the rest of the furniture in the room. No one had said anything for several minutes, possibly because none of us could think of anything that would be mutually encouraging or enlightening. Or even pleasant.

"It's just like I thought," Schoolcraft said finally, putting his feet up on the corner of his desk.

"What?" Padillo said.

"The way you two dudes acted last night. Real cool and calm. Too cool and too calm really—just like it was nothing new to get home from work and find a dead body in the living room. Or maybe the bathtub."

"We both have low blood pressure," Padillo said.

"That wasn't why they called me at six in the morning to tell me about you two."

"Tell you what?" I said.

"It wasn't so much about you, McCorkle, as it was your partner here. Did you know that you got a special kind of partner, the kind they'll bend the rules for?" Schoolcraft's tone was almost as bitter as the expression on his face. "If I remember right, they told me—not asked me—they told me to 'extend every courtesy' and to 'expedite the normal investigatory routine.' It's just like Padillo here was something more than guy who owns half a fancy gin mill."

"He's got a host of friends," I said.

"Uh-huh," Schoolcraft said and closed his eyes and massaged them with his thumb and forefinger. "Well, after I got that call, I couldn't get back to sleep. I'm not cool and calm like you two. I get sort of excitable."

I decided that he was as excitable as wallpaper.

"Well, anyway, I couldn't get back to sleep so I came on down here about seven thirty just to make sure that everyone was going to be courteous enough for you. Guess who got here five minutes later?"

"Wanda Gothar," Padillo said.

Schoolcraft didn't like Padillo's answer and he didn't seem to care whether both of us knew it. Maybe he was tired of being courteous. Or maybe he was just fed up with a job that brought him phone calls at six o'clock in the morning instructing him to be nice to persons that he didn't want to be nice to. His dark face twisted itself into a grimace that almost lapsed into a sneer. Then it relaxed and returned to its normal, expressionless pattern. It was a look that he could wear nicely to a funeral or a christening. But Schoolcraft couldn't keep the sneer out of his voice. I don't think I could have either.

"I just can't seem to come up with any surprises at all for you this morning," he said. "But seeing that you're so good at guessing, maybe you can guess what Miss Gothar wanted."

"She wanted you to give me a message," Padillo said.

Schoolcraft nodded his head several times, his eyes never leaving Padillo's face. "You know something," he said. "She reminds me of you. You two don't look anything alike, but she sort of reminds me of you. Her brother's just been killed and all and there's a couple of questions that I thought I'd like to ask her when she's still shook, you know—

such as where's she been and does she maybe have some idea about who might have wanted her brother dead. Questions like that. But before I even get my mouth set she's giving me a message to give to you."

"Wanda's like that," Padillo said. "She's always held up well under pressure."

"Well, since I didn't have any instructions to treat her special, I went ahead and asked my questions." Schoolcraft fell silent for a few moments, as if recalling the questions he'd asked and the answers he'd received. "You know how long I've been asking questions? I mean, professionally?"

"How long?" I said.

"Seventeen years. I've questioned all kinds: motherfuckers and stiff screwers and childbeaters and highgrade con artists and people who just cut up other people because they thought it was fun. You name it and I've asked about it. But I never questioned anybody like her."

"She's special all right," Padillo said.

Schoolcraft nodded and it made him look even more unhappy than before. "She wasn't shook," he said. "Not the least little bit."

"She wouldn't show it," Padillo said.

"No tears, no voice tremor, nothing. She flat refused to make a positive ID of the body, her own brother. Now with anybody else I'd say that maybe they couldn't stand the sight, you know. But with her—" Schoolcraft broke off his sentence and was silent for another moment or so as if deciding how he wanted to describe Wanda Gothar's attitude. "She just didn't really give a shit," he said finally.

"That's right," Padillo said.

Alertness flickered in Schoolcraft's dark eyes and

his nose wrinkled a couple of times as if he had just smelled something he liked. "You mean she hated her own brother—twin brother, at that?"

Padillo shook his head slightly. "They were close. Very close."

"Then why doesn't she give a shit that he's dead?"

"Because he is."

"So?"

"When somebody's dead, there's not much anyone can do about it, is there? Wanda's what might be called the ultimate realist. For her, dead is dead."

Schoolcraft moved his head slowly from side to side several times. "It's not natural." He raised his eyes to the ceiling as if thinking about what he had just said. "Maybe that's not the right word. Normal. It's not normal."

"It is for her," Padillo said.

"When I asked her where she was last night—all night—you know what she said?"

When neither of us replied, Schoolcraft looked pleased. "She said, 'Out.' That's all. Just one word, 'Out.'"

"You leaned on her pretty hard, I suppose," Padillo said.

Schoolcraft nodded. "Hard enough for nearly an hour. But all I got was that one word. Out. No explanation, no evasions, not even an apology. Just that one word." He paused to shake his head, perhaps at the wonder of it all. "Guess what she said when I asked her if she had any idea about who might have needed to kill her brother?"

"I can't," Padillo said.

"She said no. Just one word again, n-o. No. She said it fourteen times in a row because I started counting."

"You gave up on fourteen?" I said.

"I gave up at six, but went on to fourteen and then quit because all I'd get to number fifteen or sixteen or even thirty-two was that same one-word answer, no. So I didn't get much this morning, not from her, not from you, not even from the people who run this place, except some bad advice, but I can get that from them every day."

"You got something else," Padillo said.

"What?"

"A message for me."

A broad white smile split Schoolcraft's dark face. It was a boy's smile really, a happy boy, and I felt that he seldom had much cause to show it off.

"That's right," he said. "I did get that. It's some message. You ready?"

"I'm ready," Padillo said.

"She said to tell you. 'In or out by four in six-two-one.' Isn't that some message?"

"Some message," Padillo agreed.

"You got it?"

"I've got it."

"You know what it means?"

"Yes."

"But you're not going to tell me."

"No."

"You want me to tell you what it means?"

"All right."

Schoolcraft put his feet back on the floor, rose, and leaned over his desk toward Padillo. "It means that you and me will be seeing a lot more of each other."

Chapter 7

It was fifteen past when we came out of police headquarters and started walking west toward Fourth Street in search of a cab. I was about to tell Padillo that I thought I'd figured out Wanda Gothar's message, and ask whether he wanted to be dropped off at her hotel, when a green Chrysler New Yorker sedan pulled up a few feet in front of us and a man got out of the seat next to the driver.

Padillo touched my sleeve and said, "If I say go, run."

"Friends of yours?"

"Acquaintances."

The man who got out of the Chrysler wore a spade-shaped beard that was running to gray, and which almost compensated for the high gloss of his cream-colored scalp. A pair of dark glasses rested on his long white nose and his mouth seemed to be trying to smile through the beard at Padillo. He was neither tall nor short and he moved easily as if he still liked to make hard use of his body, even though it was more than fifty years old.

When he got within a few feet of us he stopped smiling long enough to say. "How are you, Padillo?" and then turned the smile back on before Padillo had the chance to reply, rotten or awful or even tolerable fair.

The only other thing I noticed about the man was

that he kept his hands motionless and in plain sight, well away from his body.

"Down to pay a traffic ticket?" Padillo said as he turned his left side to the man, his own hands relaxed, but held at belt level so that he could either block a quick left or wave for a cab.

"Actually, we were looking for you," the man said, not offering to shake hands, but still smiling when he wasn't speaking as his own hands moved slowly and carefully behind his back.

"Why?" Padillo said.

"We thought we should talk."

"About Walter Gothar?"

The man brought his hands out in sight again and used them to help him shrug. "Walter—and other things."

"Where?"

There was that smile again, a glint of white porcelain through a well-kept forest of gray and black. "You know my preference," he said.

Padillo, not taking his eyes from the man said, "Do you know a sleazy bar close by Mac? Mr. Kragstein prefers to conduct his business in them. The seedier the better."

"Sixth Street," I said. "I can think of several."

"Name one."

"The Chatterbox."

"Sleazy?"

"Foul," I said.

"Excellent," Kragstein said.

"He's coming along, you know," Padillo said, nodding his head toward me.

"Of course, of course," Kragstein murmured and turned toward the Chrysler. He opened the rear door for us. Before we got in, Padillo said, "My partner, Mr. McCorkle; Franz Kragstein."

"Hello," Kragstein said, but didn't offer to shake hands. I didn't mind. He waved toward the man at the wheel. "You know Amos, don't you, Padillo?"

"We've met," Padillo said and ducked to enter the back seat. I followed and when I'd closed the door, Padillo said, "How are you, Amos?"

The man called Amos turned slowly in the front seat to look at Padillo. He was the youngest one in the car, still in his late twenties. He looked at Padillo for a moment and then nodded to himself, as if resolving some question that had long bothered him. He looked at me next and the dismissal whipped across his face so quickly that I wasn't really sure that it had been there at all. He smiled faintly at Padillo and said, "Fine, Mike, and you?"

"Okay," Padillo said. "Mr. Gitner, Mr. McCorkle."

Amos Gitner gave me a nod before turning back to the wheel. "Where to?" he asked Kragstein.

"It's a place called The Chatterbox, on Sixth Street, I believe."

"I hope it's crummy enough for you," Gitner said.

"Mr. McCorkle assures me that it is."

The Chatterbox drew a mixed clientele in that half of the customers were drunk while the other half were trying to get that way and would soon succeed, if their money held out. We took the last booth in a row of seven that lined the left side of the room. I sat next to the wall, facing Kragstein. Padillo and Gitner, in the outside seats, faced each other across the booth's formica table top.

The Chatterbox must have been a retail store

once, a none too prosperous venture that couldn't sell enough hardware or work clothes or maybe notions. Now it sold a little food and a lot of cheap wine, beer, blended bourbon, and gin. I didn't think there was much call for Scotch.

Remodeling had been kept to the absolute minimum: there was the row of cheap booths; an L-shaped bar with a dozen or so stools; a kitchen which I could smell and had no desire to inspect; a jukebox, and a cigarette machine. I figured that the jukebox and the cigarette machine took care of the rent. The beer companies had taken care of the decorations.

There were six customers at the bar, four of them black, two of them white. No women. One of the blacks was drunk, but pleasantly so, if that's possible, and both of the whites, their necessary cigarettes all but forgotten between their fingers, had reached the point where they huddled morosely over their wine and perhaps hoped that these were the drinks that contained oblivion. Clean them up a little, find them some new clothes, and they could join the morning Bloody Mary crowd at Mac's Place and nobody would know the difference until they fell off their stools, and perhaps not even then.

The bartender was probably the owner. He wouldn't need much hired help: a relief bartender, a cook, a couple of dishwashers who could also swamp out the place, and maybe a waitress or two at noon and at night. It was a cheap place that catered to hard drinkers and the only difference between it and the saloon that I owned half of was a couple of clean shirts and a $100,000 line of credit.

"Admirable," Kragstein said, looking around.

"Really excellent. I'm surprised that you know such places, Mr. McCorkle."

"I use them to think in," I said.

Kragstein nodded approvingly as if he believed me. "I myself find them conducive for business purposes."

Before he could tell me how business was, the bartender came over, took a couple of cursory swipes at the table with a fairly clean rag, and asked us our pleasure. Kragstein's was gin. Padillo and I asked for bottled beer. Gitner wanted a Coke, perhaps because he was driving. Nobody said much until the bartender returned with the drinks. He was a stocky, dark-complexioned man, possibly a Greek, and he wasn't much impressed with his uptown trade. He served the drinks and then waited to see who would pay. They don't run tabs in places like The Chatterbox.

I kept my hands on the table and so did Padillo and when the Greek started to whistle "Carolina Moon," Kragstein got the idea and handed over a five. The bartender put $2.80 change on the table and went back to his regular customers. The same drinks in our place would have cost $1.35 more, but that's how it is with a steep overhead, which some insist on calling atmosphere.

"Well, now," Kragstein said as he peered about. "This is rather nice. But would it be possible to speak German or French?"

"Either one," Padillo said, "although McCorkle's German is better than his French."

"Then we shall speak German," Kragstein said in German and I was surprised that he spoke it with an American accent. His English was easy, but also slightly accented, although I hadn't been able to determine what flavor.

"It was too bad about Walter, wasn't it?" Kragstein said after he had taken a sip of his gin.

"Terrible," Padillo said.

"And I believe that it happened in your apartment, Mr. McCorkle."

"In the living room," I said.

"A garrote?"

"Steel wire attached to a couple of plastic bicycle handle bar grips," Padillo said, looking at Gitner. "It's supposed to be fairly popular in Southeast Asia. You spent some time out there recently, didn't you, Amos?"

"A few months," Gitner said.

"Cambodia, wasn't it?"

"There and a couple of other places."

"Free-lance or contract?"

"Does it matter?"

"I heard it was contract."

"Believe anything you like, Padillo, as long as it's comforting."

Gitner wasn't a tall man, but he had nice moves. I hadn't seen him smoke and if he drank nothing but Coca-Cola, his teeth might have a few fillings, but there was nothing wrong with his liver. He looked American—the way young, earnest Americans looked a decade or so ago before they discovered things that they thought were more important than close shaves, clean fingernails, tidy haircuts and J. Press suits. Gitner was something of an anachronism, I decided, a throwback to the fifties with his crew cut light brown hair, his quiet tweed jacket, his expensive gray flannel trousers, his buttondown white shirt, the marble-sized knot in his red silk tie, and his burnished cordovan oxfords. I tried to decide whom he reminded me of and it came as faint surprise when I realized that Gitner was a blond version of Padillo as he'd been not quite fifteen years ago when I'd first met him, before he'd let his sideburns reach his earlobes and before he'd cultivated the moustache that I thought made him look like the Dark Knight from Iberia, a little down on his luck perhaps, but ready for either fight or frolic. But that's what I get for having been reared on Tennyson.

"I thought we should clear the air about a few things, Michael," Kragstein said and waved his right hand around as if to demonstrate what he meant.

"Go ahead," Padillo said.

"Am I to understand that you intend to lend your talents to Miss Gothar, now that her brother is dead?"

"I've been thinking about it."

"Not out of sentiment, surely?"

"No."

Kragstein nodded, as if reassured by Padillo's answer. "Good," he said and paused for another sip of gin. "We are, as you've probably gathered, interested in one Peter Paul Kassim."

"So I've heard."

"And you, too, are interested in him."

"Only in his health."

"As are we."

Padillo said nothing. Instead he borrowed a cigarette from me, lit it with his own matches, and blew some smoke up into the air, gazing around the bar as if wondering how much it would cost to buy in.

"Perhaps I should first assure you that we are in

no manner responsible for Walter Gothar's death. I hope you believe me."

"Sure," Padillo said. "But would it make any difference if I didn't?"

"None," Gitner said. "None at all."

"Walter seemed a little worried about you, Amos. He thought you had him in your book."

"Did he say that?"

"More or less."

"He was wrong."

"That won't bother him now."

Gitner tasted his Coca-Cola as if he expected it to have turned sour. From the look on his face, it may have. He put it down and shoved it away from him toward Kragstein. "Gothar wasn't as good as he thought he was," he said. "That's why he's dead."

"He was pretty good," Padillo said. "Personally, I thought he was too good to let somebody get behind him with a garrote."

"Maybe it was his sister," Gitner said. "It sounds like her."

"Maybe," Padillo said.

"I thought you had a thing going with her."

"That was a few years back."

"What happened?"

"Do you feel it's vital that you know?"

Gitner smiled, but it wasn't a pleasant one. I felt that he may not have had any other kind. "You're not letting me needle you, are you, Padillo?"

"I don't think so."

"Good. I just want to make sure that if something happens to Wanda, you won't let feel any great personal loss."

"None," Padillo said. "But whoever gets to her might have to go through me."

Gitner nodded slowly, more to himself than to anyone else. "That could be interesting," he said. "That could be real interesting."

"Wanda has told you about Kassim, of course," Kragstein said comfortably.

"She hasn't told me anything except that she's got a client you've taken an order on."

"I thought you said—"

Padillo interrupted him. "I said that I'd heard that you were interested in Kassim and that I'm concerned about his health. That's all. The rest of it you assumed."

"But this arrangement of yours with the Gothars. It would—"

"There's no arrangement."

"Are you trying to cut yourself in or out, Padillo?" Gitner said.

"I'm already in. The only question left is for how much and who's going to pay it."

Gitner and Kragstein traded glances, meaningful ones, I assumed. Kragstein decided to do the talking, probably because he was better at it. "We could always work out an accommodation, Michael."

"What kind?"

"We've accepted this assignment on an incentive arrangement. The young man is to sign certain papers as soon as his brother dies. If he does not sign those papers, we receive a sizable bonus. Our fee is still adequate if he does sign the papers, but does not return to Llaquah. We receive virtually nothing if he does sign the papers and returns to Llaquah."

"So you're in a hurry," Padillo said.

"That's right," Gitner said. "We're in a hurry."

"Who's your client?"

"Does that matter?" Kragstein asked.

"It does to McCorkle."

"Really? How?"

"He was hoping it would be the wicked uncle."

"Kassim doesn't have any uncles," Gitner said.

"Cousins?" I said, trying to make my voice sound hopeful.

"He's got some aunts and some cousins, but no uncles, except by marriage."

"I don't suppose they count," I said.

Gitner turned to Kragstein. "What's he talking about?"

"We were discussing the possibility of working out an accommodation with Padillo before we became sidetracked," Kragstein said. "Shall we continue?"

"Fine," Padillo said.

Kragstein nodded. "We could arrange it several ways, of course, Michael. The one I prefer is that you come to your understanding with Miss Gothar and then be not nearly as proficient as you usually are."

"In other words, you take a dive," Gitner said.

"For how much?" Padillo said.

Kragstein pointed the end of his beard at the dirty ceiling. "Oh, say twenty-five thousand. Dollars, of course."

"And I'd also be expected to tip you off about where Kassim might be stashed away," Padillo said.

"Yes," Kragstein said. "That would be expected."

"All for twenty-five thousand dollars."

"That's right," Gitner said. "Twenty-five thousand. That's good money for doing what you'd be doing which is nothing. I'd like to make twenty-five big ones for doing nothing."

"How much front money?" Padillo said.

Kragstein ran a thick, nicely cared for hand over his gleaming scalp before answering. "Possibly seventy-five hundred."

Padillo laughed. It wasn't really a laugh, it was more of a sharp, wordless bark of contempt. "Both you and Wanda," he said.

"Both of us what?" Kragstein said.

"You're both working on spec. How much oil do they guess is underneath Llaquah—eighty billion barrels?"

"Ninety," Kragstein said.

Padillo leaned toward him across the table and switched from German to English. "That means a country whose annual income has been hovering around zero will get to watch it shoot up to seven or eight hundred million dollars a year—which is more than Kuwait gets. But that's all sweet bye and bye money. Right now there's not enough hard cash in this deal on either side to buy a pack of cigarettes."

"The money will be there," Kragstein said.

"What's your asking price, Franz, a quarter of a million?"

"That's close enough," Gitner said.

"And you're offering me ten percent, except that all you can scrape up between you in front money is seventy-five hundred. That means that you're both almost broke and that's why you've taken it on spec—because there's nothing better around."

"You're not rejecting our offer, are you, Padillo?" Kragstein said in a new soft low tone that made what he'd said sound more like a threat than a question.

Padillo rose. "That's right," he said. "Maybe your

new partner doesn't know that I've never worked on the cheap, Franz, but you do."

"I've heard that about you, Padillo," Gitner said. "That and a lot of other things. Maybe now I can find out if some of them are true."

I was standing by Padillo now as he looked down at Amos Gitner. He looked at him steadily for several moments before he shifted his gaze to Kragstein.

"Maybe you'd better tell him, Franz," he said. "Somebody should."

"Tell him what?"

"That he's not all that good."

Kragstein did something with his mouth so that his teeth showed through the thicket of his beard. It could have been a smile. "I think he is," he said.

"You're talking about technique, aren't you?"

"Of course."

"Then you forgot something."

"What?"

"Brains," Padillo said. "He hasn't got enough."

Chapter 8

Outside I waved at a Diamond cab but he sailed on by after looking us over carefully. It may have been that he didn't care for the cut of my forest green cavalry twill suit, the double-breasted one that caused kindly friends to ask whether I hadn't lost a few pounds. Or it may have been that the black scowl on Padillo's face bothered him. It would have bothered me.

"Smile, for Christ's sake," I said, "or start walking."

Padillo pulled his lips back and showed his teeth. "It hurts," he said.

"It was just like in the movies," I said, waving at a Yellow cab whose driver nodded cheerfully at me as he drove on past.

"How?"

"A Western," I said. "Old Gunfighter, living on nothing but his reputation, drifts into End-of-the-line, New Mexico, slapping the alkali dust from his chaps—"

"End-of-the-line's good."

"And runs into none other than Big Rancher's only son who's craving to get out from under Daddy's shadow and make it on his own."

"So Only Son challenges Old Gunfighter to a showdown."

"You've seen it," I said as an Independent cab rolled to a stop in front of us.

"I never could sit through to the end," Padillo said as he climbed in. "How does it turn out?"

"Sad," I said and told the driver that we wanted to go to the Hay-Adams Hotel.

"You know how I'd end it?" Padillo said.

"How?"

"I'd have Old Gunfighter wait for a moonless night and then sneak quietly out of town."

"You may be the last of the romantics, Mike."

"How'd you know I wanted to go to the Hay-Adams?"

"Wanda Gothar's message. I figured it out. I think."

"'In or out by four in six-two-one.'"

"That means you're supposed to make up your mind by four o'clock today. She's in room six-twenty-one. I can also do large sums in my head."

"You're a comfort."

"What're you going to tell her?"

"That I'm in."

"How do you think she really took her brother's death?"

"Hard," he said and then looked at me. "You're actually curious, aren't you?"

"I get that way about people who're killed in my own living room," I said and hoped that the cab-driver was enjoying the conversation.

"So now you want to see act two?"

"Only if it doesn't drag."

"For some reason," Padillo said, "I don't think it will."

The Hay-Adams is a middle-aged hotel on Sixteenth Street right across from Lafayette Square where they recently went to a lot of trouble to build some new sidewalks and trash baskets for the crowds who gathered under the trees to say nasty things about the war in Indochina, pollution, the economy, and the man who lived in the big white house on Pennsylvania Avenue across the street from the square. The crowds and what they said must not have bothered the man much because up until then he hadn't done a great deal about the things that they complained about.

We took an elevator up to the sixth floor. Padillo knocked twice on 621 and Wanda Gothar's voice asked, "Who is it?" before she opened the door after Padillo identified himself.

She nearly winced when she saw me, but all that she said was, "Still the mute witness, Mr. McCorkle?"

"I speak up from time to time."

After we were in the room she turned to Padillo. "Well?"

"I'm in."

"How much?"

"How much can you afford?"

"Fifty thousand, plus ten thousand for whoever killed my brother."

"Just the name?"

"Just the name."

"Amos Gitner thinks you might have done it."

"That's not worth ten thousand."

"I didn't think it would be. How much front money, Wanda?"

She looked away from him and ran her left forefinger up and down the dark blue material that made up the pants of her suit. "Five thousand."

"Business must be bad all over. Kragstein and Gitner could only offer me seventy-five hundred and from what I hear, they've been working regularly."

"We took it on a contingency basis."

"So did they."

She turned back to him and when she spoke her voice was low and level and very hard. "Just get me that name and you've got the ten thousand, Padillo, even if it takes every last cent I've got." She turned away again, as if the melodrama of the statement embarrassed her. "What did Kragstein and Gitner say?"

"That they didn't kill Walter."

"What else?"

"That they get a bonus if Kassim doesn't sign certain papers. No bonus if he does sign, but doesn't make it back to Llaquah."

"A sliding scale," she said. "Did they mention who's paying them?"

"No."

"Did you ask?"

"Yes."

"And you turned them down?"

"That's right."

"What did they say?"

"Not much."

"Gitner must have said something."

"He seemed to think that I'm getting old."

She inspected him carefully, much as she might inspect a cold-storage chicken that had been a trifle long in the freezer. "You are, you know."

"Everybody is," Padillo said.

"Well, does the five thousand hold you?"

"Forget it."

"What do you mean, forget it? What are we playing now, Padillo, one of your clever little games?"

"No games. I'm in for free and if I find out who killed Walter, you get that for nothing, too."

"I don't like anything when it's free," she said. "If it's a gift horse, I look in its mouth. Since it's from you, I might even ask for X rays."

"Don't."

"Why?"

"Because," he said, "you might find out how old and tired he really is."

Wanda Gothar's room wasn't the best that the Hay-Adams had to offer, nor was it the worse. The view from the two windows was mostly of AFL-CIO headquarters, which was across Sixteenth Street, and the room was furnished with a double bed, a few chairs, a combination dresser-writing table, and the inevitable television set. It was a commercial traveler's room, one to sleep in for a couple of nights, three at the most, before hastening back home or on to the next town. From the looks of the room she could have been there for an hour or for a month because there was nothing in it that seemed to belong to her. No suitcase, no cosmetic kit, nor even a box of Kleenex or a paperback book. I decided that she was either a highly experienced traveler or a compulsive neatener, one of those who gag at the sight of a crushed-out cigarette in an ashtray.

She was turned toward the windows, her back to Padillo and me, when she said. "All right. When do you start?"

"As soon as you give me some answers," he said.

"Such as?"

"Why did you fake the note from Paul?"

She turned from the window and made a small gesture with her left hand, as if the question were hardly worth an answer. "We were almost broke and we needed help. The only way we landed this assignment was by assuring them that you'd be in on it. You and Paul had been close and we thought that you might feel something—a sentimental obligation perhaps. That was dumb of us."

"You should've remembered that I knew he didn't read or write English."

She shrugged. "It was a chance we took. Not many knew it because he spoke it perfectly. He had that block, which for some reason kept him from either reading or writing it. Walter forged his handwriting."

"He was always good at that," Padillo said.

"That and other things."

"It still doesn't make sense."

"Why?"

"You could have written it in German just as easily. Whose idea was it to write in English?"

She turned back to the window. "Mine."

"Because you didn't really want me in, did you, Wanda?"

"No. You don't have to ask why, do you?"

"No, I don't think so."

"It's different now," she said as she turned, walked across the room to a straight-backed chair, and lowered herself onto it in the easy, graceful way that they once taught in the better finishing schools.

"How?" Padillo said.

"I need you," she said, gazing at the gray carpet. She stared at it a moment before looking up. "I don't like admitting it, but I do. I'm the last of the Gothars. That doesn't mean anything to anyone other than me, but I'd like to stay alive. Did you hear how Paul was killed in Beirut?"

"No," Padillo said. "I just heard that it was messy."

"His throat was cut."

"That's hard to believe."

She nodded. "It is, isn't it? He was good, wasn't he?"

"I'd say he was almost the best."

"Which means that it was somebody he knew. And trusted."

"As much as he'd trust anyone," Padillo said.

"The same thing must have happened to Walter. He was no easy mark either."

"Why was your brother in my apartment?" I said.

She shook her head twice. "I don't know. He was supposed to have been with them."

"Who's them?" Padillo said.

"Kassim and Scales. You don't know about Scales, do you?"

"No."

"He knows about you. He hired us on the condition that you'd be part of things."

"I still don't know him."

"Emory Scales. He was Kassim's tutor until the boy went into the monastery."

"English?"

"Yes."

"And now he's what?"

"He's Kassim's adviser."

"And just popped up after Kassim's brother had the car wreck?"

"Kassim sent for him, I understand."

"And Scales got in touch with you."

"Yes."

"What's he been doing recently? I mean was he

still in Llaquah or back in England when Kassim sent for him?"

"He was back in England," she said.

"You mentioned that Walter was supposed to have been with them when he came visiting McCorkle. I assume that means they're here in Washington."

Wanda Gothar shook her head again. "Baltimore."

Padillo rose from the room's one easy chair and walked over to the window. "Why would he want to see McCorkle?"

"I don't know," she said.

"Guess."

"Maybe he thought that he could persuade McCorkle to persuade you."

"That's thin."

"Have you got something better?"

"Not yet. What do Kassim and Scales say?"

"About what?"

"Come on, Wanda."

"They don't say anything about why he left them in Baltimore. They said he told them that he had an appointment and that he'd be back and that they should remain where they were."

"And where's that?"

"It doesn't matter," she said. "I'm moving them."

"When?"

"As soon as Kassim's brother dies."

"What's the latest report?" Padillo asked.

"He's still in a coma."

"Where're you moving them to?"

She looked at Padillo and then at me. "There's nothing in it for McCorkle," Padillo said.

"Perhaps that's what worries me," she said.

"There could be something in it for me," I said.

"What?" she said.

"I'd like to know why your brother got killed in my apartment. So would the police. They'll stop bothering me as soon as they find out who killed him and why. The quicker they find out, the better I'll like it."

"Where're you moving them to, Wanda?" Padillo said.

"To New York first," she said.

"Then where?"

She looked at Padillo for nearly fifteen seconds. It was a searching, suspicious look such as she might give the two-carat diamond ring that could be had for only fifty dollars along with a touching hard luck story. "I don't think you should know that just yet," she said.

"All right," he said, "you can tell me something else."

"What?"

"Where were you last night when your brother was being garroted?"

"You really think you need to know, don't you?"

"I think so."

"It's just as I told the police," she said. "I was out."

"You'll have to do better than that," Padillo said.

"I didn't for the police."

"You'll have to for me."

They exchanged another long look. "I was out with a man," she said finally.

"Where?"

"In his bed. Actually, it's only partly his. The rest of it belongs to his wife."

"What is he?" Padillo said.

She turned to me. "Notice that he said what, not who. That's what persons are to him. Things."

"Like chess pieces," I said.

"No," she said, "more like the game you call checkers. All counters have the same value."

"He's a true democrat," I said.

"He asked what the man is because he wants to know how much the man has to lose if he eventually becomes my alibi. If he's a bellhop or a taxi driver, then he has little to lose. A wife, perhaps, but he can always get another, can't he, Padillo?"

"He's Government, isn't he, Wanda?"

"Yes, damn it, he's Government."

"I may have to have his name."

"What will you do with it, blackmail him?"

Padillo smiled at her, but it wasn't the kind of a smile that one returns. "No," he said, "I'll merely use it to make sure of something."

"Of what?"

"Not much. Just that you're not lying."

Chapter 9

It was collect, of course. That's the only kind of long-distance call I ever get at three o'clock in the morning and often as not it's from someone I haven't seen in fifteen years and haven't thought of in ten. Usually, they just want to talk because they're about three-fourths of the way through a bottle of bourbon and the wife has gone to bed and it seems like a damned good idea to call up old McCorkle and find out how the hell he is.

But sometimes they've run into a little trouble and need fifty dollars to get out of jail or a hundred to get to the next town where the new job is waiting and they can't think of anybody else in the whole world who'll lend it to them except me and please, for Christ's sake, would I mind wiring it?

So I usually send the money because it's as cheap a way as I can think of to make sure they they don't call anymore. After I hang up I sometimes lie there in bed and try to think of whom I could call at three in the morning to send me fifty or a hundred. It's not a long list.

This time it was Padillo and he was calling from New York and after I told the operator that I'd accept the call, I said, "How much do you need?"

"I've got a little trouble."

"It's not so little if you're calling at three in the morning."

"They made a try about two hours ago."

"Where?"
"In Delaware," Padillo said. "I was driving them up."
"From Baltimore?"
"Right."
"Was it Kragstein and Gitner?"
"It must have been, but it was too dark to tell."
"What happened?"
"They pulled up alongside and tried."
"Tried?"
"I caught on in time and they went off the road."
"Anyone hurt?"
"You mean them or us?"
"Us," I said. "You."
"No. Kassim was barely ruffled."
"What about the other guy, his adviser?"
"Scales? He's another cucumber."
"So what do you need?"
"Another hand."
"Who?"
"Do you remember one of our customers called William Plomondon?"
"I see his trucks around town. Plomondon the Plumber. He's a pretty big contractor."
"Call him for me first thing tomorrow."
"What'll I tell him, that the sink's stopped up?"
"Invite him to lunch. He won't take it over the phone. Tell him that I can use him for three days in New York and that there'll be a bonus."
"He'll know what I'm talking about?"
I could hear Padillo's rare sigh. It wasn't one of impatience. It was one of weariness that may have contained a touch of regret. "He'll know."
"Where'll I tell him to call you?"

"No calls," Padillo said. "I'm using a phone booth."

"What's the address?"

It was on Avenue A in Manhattan and I remembered the neighborhood. It would never win any prizes in the annual Spring paint-up, fix-up campaign.

"You're right downtown," I said. "When do you want him to show?"

"By seven o'clock tonight."

"And you really need him?"

"I really need him."

"What happened to Wanda?"

"That's why I need him. She'll be gone for three days and after that I'll have to move Kassim and Scales again."

"Any idea where?"

"West, I think," he said. "but where west I don't know."

"Was Wanda with you when Gitner and Kragstein made their try?"

"No. She left as soon as she got the news."

"What news?"

"Kassim's older brother."

"What about him?"

"He died six hours ago. The kid is now king."

"Give him my congratulations," I said

"I'll do that," Padillo said and hung up.

Padillo had been gone for nearly two days when he called me at three Friday morning. I'd last seen him at the Hay-Adams, still negotiating his uneasy truce with Wanda Gothar. Since then I'd kept fairly busy at the none too arduous tasks that compose saloonkeeping. If it had been hard work, I'd have gone into something else. But I'd signed some purchase orders; hired a new pastry chef who claimed to make a remarkable kirsch torte; turned down the Muzak salesman for the ninth time; approved a recommendation by Herr Horst to buy some new uniforms for the waiters and busboys, and had a fairly friendly, explorative talk with the business agent for Local 781 of the Hotel and Restaurant Employees and Bartenders International Union (AFL-CIO) who thought I should be paying the help a little more money. I told him that I thought they should be working a little harder, so we left it at that for the time being and had a drink and talked about the kind of restaurant he planned to open once he got out of what he described as the "labor game."

After Padillo called I'd made the late luncheon date with William Plomondon and I was sitting at the bar waiting for him when Karl moved down to my end and started rearranging some glasses that didn't much need it.

"What's new?" I said.

"The duchess was in the bag again," he said.

"That's not new."

"I thought you'd like to know."

She wasn't really a duchess. She was the wife of a cabinet member with whom I'd finally had to have a little chat because the Mrs. insisted on having lunch at our place at least twice a week, which was all right, except that she usually drank it and needed help to make it out the front door. We'd come to an arrangement so that whenever she showed up Herr Horst would call a certain number in the cabinet member's office and a departmental limousine would be dispatched to take her home or on to her next appointment. She drank straight double vodkas and Padillo predicted that she would wake up in a drying-out place within three months. I gave her six and Karl, less tolerant or perhaps more realistic, claimed that she had only a few weeks left.

"How big was her party?" I said.

"Five other broads. Nobody important. The duchess is supposed to show at the Spanish Embassy reception tonight, but I don't think she'll make it. If she does, she'll probably jump in the goldfish pool again."

Karl had worked for Padillo and me in Bonn where he'd been bored by both the Bundestag and whatever passed for social life in that village on the Rhine. Although I found it difficult to decide which of the capital cities was duller, Karl thought that Washington glittered and regarded Congress as an endless drama. He was on a first-name basis with at least fifty Representatives and a dozen Senators, knew how the rest of them voted on every issue, was a primary source of backstairs gossip for half of the town's society reporters, and was occasionally consulted by a couple of syndicated columnists who also put great faith in the philosophical pronunciamentos of New York cabdrivers. In addition, Karl was also the best bartender in town. Padillo had seen to that.

"When's Mike coming back?" he said.

"In a couple of days."

"Where is he?"

"Out of town."

"I was hoping I could talk to you guys about something."

I sighed and turned from my vigil at the door. Plomondon could find me easily enough when he arrived. I had a more important problem. My bartender wanted to borrow some money.

"What barn did you find it in?" I said.

"You'll never believe it."

"That'll make it easier to say no."

"Listen," Karl said and patted a stray lock of long blond hair back into place, I think he may have pioneered the trend because he'd worn it long for more than a dozen years. "It's a Dues."

"You can't afford a Duesenberg," I said. "Nobody can."

"It's a 1934 blown SJ with a Rollston body."

"What kind of shape is it in?" I said, getting interested in spite of myself.

"Cherry."

In addition to being the town tattle, Karl was also a classic car buff. He'd owned a series of them beginning with a 1939 Lincoln Continental that I'd found for him in Copenhagen. He'd keep one awhile and then sell it for a respectable profit in what seemed to be a steadily rising market. I didn't share his passion, but after all, they'd only made 500 of the things, and he probably wanted this one so much that it hurt.

"How much?" I said.

Karl busied himself with the glasses again. "Twenty-five," he said in a voice so low that it was hard to decide whether it was a whisper or a whimper.

"Jesus," I said.

"Look," he said, whipping out a ballpoint pen and using a paper napkin to figure on. "I know where I can get fifteen tomorrow for the Hispano-Suiza." That's what he was then driving. "I got five saved so really all I need is another five."

"It doesn't make sense," I said. "Twenty-five

thousand dollars for a car that's nearly forty years old."

"It'll be worth thirty-five easy in less'n five years."

"It's in good shape?" I said, feeling myself weakening and hating it.

"Perfect."

"I'll talk to Padillo when he gets back."

"This guy can't hold it forever."

"When Mike gets back."

"I'll call the guy and tell him I'll take it."

"Look, I didn't say—"

"I think your lucheon date's here," Karl said.

I turned and watched Plomondon the Plumber move across the room toward the bar. He was a small, compact man, not quite forty and not over five-five who walked on the balls of his feet and swung his arms a little more than necessary, something like a British soldier who's never off parade. He had brown curly hair that was cut close to his head, which may have been a little too big for his body, but which he carried at a proud angle with chin out and shoulders back.

He nodded at me as he came and when he was close enough he stuck out his hand and said. "I'm Bill Plomondon."

I shook his hand, which was dry and hard and also too large for the rest of him, and said that I was glad to see him and asked whether he would prefer to have lunch in a private room.

"I like things out in the open."

I nodded and turned to survey the dining room. It was a little past two because Plomondon had said he couldn't make it any earlier so there were several tables available. I caught Herr Horst's eye and he nodded and glided across the room toward us.

"Number eighteen, I think, Herr Horst," I said.

"Of course, Herr McCorkle," he said with the stiff formality that we'd both maintained in private as well as public for nearly fifteen years.

We could have squeezed another ten tables into the dining room and perhaps no one would have complained, but a lot of our customers ate with us because we kept the tables far enough apart so that they could describe their latest triumphs and disasters in a normal conversational tone without fear of being overheard.

When we were seated, Plomondon waved away the menu. "I'd like a small steak rare and a salad. If you're having a drink, I'll take a martini any way that they like to make it."

To celebrate this no-nonsense approach I ordered the same thing and when the drinks came, he took a sip, put it down, folded his arms on the table, leaned forward and stared at me with brown eyes that didn't seem overly impressed with what the world had to offer.

"How's Mike?" he said.

"All right."

Plomondon shook his head. "If he was all right, he wouldn't have you inviting me for lunch."

"He said he can use you in New York for three days and that there'd be a bonus."

Plomondon didn't nod or frown or do anything other than blink at me twice with those seen-it-all eyes of his. "No," he said. "Tell him that. No."

"He said he needed you by seven tonight."

"It's still no."

"All right," I said.

Plomondon moved his head to look first right and then left and then over his shoulder. He had a small face for the size of his head. There was a great deal of forehead and chin and they seemed to have shoved his mouth, nose and eyes together into a neat, compact area that could be easily attended to. His nose tilted up at its end and his mouth didn't have much upper lip which made him look as if he pouted a lot, although I don't think he really did. When he was satisfied that nobody was eaves-dropping, he leaned forward again and said, "You don't talk about it a lot, do you?"

"About what?"

"About Padillo and what he does."

"He runs a saloon," I said.

"Good. I run a plumbing company. A big one."

"I've seen your trucks."

"I also take on the odd job now and then. Not often. Just now and then. So you see I've got my lines out."

After that he didn't say anything for a while. We sat there sipping our drinks until the steaks came. Plomondon cut his up all at once into precise one-inch cubes which he proceeded to eat in a methodical manner, giving each cube twenty-five chews. I became so fascinated I counted. When he was through with the steak, he polished off the salad, cutting it up into manageable squares with knife and fork. I didn't bother to count how many times he chewed his lettuce.

Herr Horst was keeping an eye on us and when we were through eating, the coffee was served promptly. Mac's Place is the only restaurant in the world where I get decent service. In others I seem to turn invisible. But Plomondon seemed no more impressed by the service than he had been by the food. I felt that he would have been just as happy eating fried cat as long as it came in one-inch cubes.

When he'd finished his first cup of coffee he again leaned forward, signaling that he had something important to say. First, he nodded his head a couple of times. "Nice lunch," he said.

"Thanks."

"I eat here quite a bit."

"I know."

"To eat here regular you've either got to have a lot of money or a loose expense account."

"We planned it that way."

"Yeah. Well, when I started out in the plumbing business right after Korea I couldn't afford to eat in places like this. Sometimes I couldn't even afford a White Tower."

"A lot of people had to struggle at first."

"You didn't," he said and before I could say how did he know, he went on. "I can look at a guy and tell whether he's been hard up against it. You think I'm kidding? I can look at you and tell that you're the kind of a guy who'd say screw it if you had to eat in a White Tower and then go and do something else. Maybe that's why you went into the restaurant business, so you'd never have to eat in a White Tower."

"Maybe," I said, "but I've eaten in them."

"But not because you had to."

"It was my own choice."

"That's what I thought. When I first started out in the plumbing business I got a little impatient too. I wanted it big right away, but it doesn't work like that unless you got the capital. So I put some lines out and started taking on the odd job now and then. I did pretty much what Padillo once did except that I didn't stick to government work exclusively, if you know what I mean."

I told him that I did and he nodded and said, "I'm still not saying anything, not anything important anyhow, but those odd jobs provided the expansion capital I needed. Now I don't really need the outside work, but that's not why I'm saying no to Padillo."

"Why then?"

"He and I don't owe each other anything. We never worked together. But I know about him and he knows about me and I always figured if I really needed somebody, I maybe could call him in. Maybe. I guess he figured the same way."

"I guess he did."

"Well, like I said, I've still got my lines out and I think I know what Padillo's on and who he's up against and I don't want any part of it. No hard feelings, understand?"

"I think so."

"Amos Gitner," he said quickly and watched my face closely for its reaction. There must have been some because he smiled for the first time. "I was pretty certain," he said. "Now I'm sure."

"That it's Gitner?"

Plomondon shook his head. "That I don't want any part of it."

He rose then and held out his hand and said, "Tell Padillo I'm sorry we couldn't do business." I shook his hand and he turned away, but turned back and leaned on the table, his large head thrust toward me. "Maybe you'd better tell him the real reason, too," he said.

"All right."

"Tell him," he said slowly, "that I'm not good

enough anymore." He paused, as if thinking of something he wanted to add, but wasn't sure whether he really should. Finally, he said, "Tell him that I hope he is."

"I'll tell him."

Plomondon seemed satisfied that I would and nodded at me in a friendly fashion before he turned and headed for the door and out into the world where there were now enough stuffed-up toilets so that he no longer had to eat at the White Tower.

I walked slowly back to the office and sat behind the partners' desk for a while. After a few minutes I took down a two-year-old copy of the *World Almanac* and looked up Llaquah. The *Almanac* said that Llaquah was under British protection until it became independent in 1959, that it had nearly a third of the free world's estimated oil reserves, that it was an absolute monarchy, that it was destined to become one of the richest nations in the world, at least on a per capita basis, and that it had a standing army of 2,000.

I put the *World Almanac* back on the shelf and sat there at the desk, admiring my view of the alley. I looked at my watch and saw that it was nearly three. I continued to sit there, thinking of Llaquah and speculating about how its citizens were going to spend all that oil money. I also wondered who had used the garrote on Walter Gothar and why they'd chosen my apartment, and pondered the capricious fate that had turned me into a saloonkeeper, and then tried to figure out what income tax bracket we would be elevated into if Fredl got the raise that she intended to demand, and finally wondered how badly Padillo really needed Plomondon the

Plumber who thought he was no longer good enough to cope with the likes of Amos Gitner. I thought about that last for quite a while and when I looked at my watch again it was nearly four.

I got up and went over to one of the three filing cabinets and opened a drawer that was labeled Miscellaneous. It contained a small transistor radio whose batteries had gone dead, a pair of binoculars that some customer had left and never returned for, an emergency bottle of Scotch which Padillo had described as ridiculous, and a .38-caliber Smith & Wesson revolver with a one-inch barrel which I took out and dropped into an attaché case that contained two shirts, two pairs of shorts, some socks, a tie that I'd never really liked, and some toilet articles. I snapped the attaché case shut and used the phone to ask Herr Horst whether he could see me for a moment.

When he came into the office I said in German. "I am joining Herr Padillo in New York for a few days."

"Very good, sir."

"Take care of things."

"Of course, sir."

"Check out the new pastry chef."

"With great care."

"Do we have five hundred in the till?"

"I believe so."

"Get it for me and I'll fill out a cash voucher."

When Herr Horst returned with the money I handed him the voucher. He politely followed me through the restaurant and to the front door which he held open. He bowed slightly and said, "Have a good journey. Herr McCorkle." I looked at him, but there was nothing in his manner or on his face but polite, frozen reserve. If I'd told him that I wanted to burn the place down, he would have handed me the matches.

I thanked him and went out into the street and flagged a cab, cheering the driver a little when I told him that I wanted to go to National Airport.

As doughty McCorkle went rushing to the rescue down Seventeenth Street in his hired hack he remembered that he'd forgotten something. He'd forgotten to pack the bullets. That made him feel a bit foolish all the way out to the airport, but it was a feeling that seemed in perfect harmony with the rest of what he'd done that day.

Chapter 10

I thought I'd lost them. They'd seemed clumsy at first, but later I decided that they weren't clumsy at all, only indifferent about whether I knew that they were following me. They weren't trying to hide, not with those twin blue blazers and those checked trousers and those pink shirts. Their ties were different though. The tall, muscular one with the thin dark face and the horseshoe moustache wore a dark red one that had a big knot and looked like satin. The other man, a little shorter, but not much, fair and almost pale, wore a purple and red striped tie that clashed with the pink of his shirt. At least I thought it clashed. He may have planned it that way.

They probably had followed me from the restaurant, but I was never sure. I didn't notice them until I got in line for the Eastern shuttle. I tried to be last in line. I always do because it's rumored that if Eastern doesn't have a seat for you on its regular shuttle to New York, it will roll out a special plane just for you. I'd like that. That's why I always try to be last in line. I kept hanging back, but so did they and finally, when it was obvious that there were plenty of seats and there wasn't a chance of getting a plane all for myself, I handed over the yellow boarding pass and walked out to the airliner which I think was a DC-9, but I wasn't sure. The new jets are as indistinguishable to me as the new cars.

I went as far back into the plane as I could, hoping that the blue blazers would have to sit in front of me. They did—one seat up and on the other side of the aisle so that I could admire their profiles all the way to LaGuardia.

The dark one looked to be twenty-seven or so with a pronounced overbite that his droopy moustache didn't do anything for. He had thick eyebrows and a beaked nose and was dark enough to be from either Cuba or Mexico. The fair one kept chewing on something, either gum or his tongue. He had a lot of freckles which not many persons seem to have anymore. Or perhaps I don't notice them. The fair one was also around twenty-seven and wore dark glasses and occasionally picked his pink nose. They both wore their hair long enough to obscure part of their ears and their coat collars and neither of them even glanced at me all the way to New York.

The first thing I did when I got off the plane was to head for the men's room where I paid seventy-five cents for a shine. They both wore suede desert boots so they had to hang around and pretend not to watch until I was through. Then I headed for the Avis counter and rented a car. That wasn't covered by their instructions and they held a hurried conference before deciding that one of them should go find a cab while the other kept an eye on me.

The car that I rented was a Plymouth. I know because I looked at its emblem to make sure. I took a deep breath, started the engine, and headed out into New York's six o'clock traffic, an act of bravery that deserved some kind of a medal. In the rear-view mirror I could see the cab containing the blue blazers right behind me.

I decided on the Triborough Bridge, not because it was a quicker route, but because it promised the most traffic. I made use of it. I switched lanes a dozen times, slowed down and speeded up, and faked a couple of turnoffs. The tailing cab stayed right with me. On FDR Drive I stuck to the right-hand lane and turned off on Sixty-third Street. Traffic got snarled and we crept along, averaging something like three miles per hour.

Sixty-third is one-way and between Lexington and Park I found what I was looking for: a double-parked delivery truck. I pulled up parallel with the truck and killed my engine. Leaving the keys in the ignition, I opened the left-hand door and got out, carrying my attaché case. I raised the Plymouth's hood, shook my head, turned, and left it there in the middle of the street for the Avis people and the New York traffic cops to worry about. I headed up Sixty-third toward Park. By the time I turned the corner, the maddened drivers who were stuck behind the abandoned car were leaning on their horns. I could also hear a few coarse shouts. I looked back just once and the two men in blue blazers were out of their cab, but still involved in some kind of an argument with its driver.

On Sixty-second and Park I got lucky and found a cab discharging a passenger. The driver was more or less willing to take me to the Biltmore and during the ride, I kept looking back, but the traffic was too heavy to be sure that I'd lost them, but I thought I had. The driver let me out on the Forty-third Street side of the Biltmore. I wandered about its red and gold lobby for fifteen minutes and when I spotted neither of them I went down the stairs and out the Forty-fourth Street entrance. After a quarter of an hour I caught another cab and gave the address on Avenue A.

When we were three blocks away from where I wanted to go I told the driver to stop. He pulled up in front of a bar and I paid him and went inside. The bar was on Second Avenue and it was crowded. The clock above the bottles said six forty-five. I ordered a Scotch and water and stood at the bar, watching the door.

I spent ten minutes in the bar and then I went out into the street and started walking toward Avenue A. I turned the corner at Ninth Street and First Avenue and the taller one with the heavy moustache hit me on the right arm with what felt like a blackjack.

As I said, I thought I'd lost them, but I hadn't. I dropped the attaché case and backed off. I wanted to rub my right arm because it ached and when I moved it, it hurt even worse. The smaller one came at me first, low and with his left hand stiff and well-extended. I assumed he was some kind of karate devotee, possibly self-taught, so I kicked his left kneecap and when he yelled and grabbed for it, I hit him just below his right ear with my left fist. I hit him hard and he sat down on the sidewalk and held his kneecap and yelled some more. I turned toward the taller one who was bringing the blackjack around and down in an arc and it seemed to whistle as it came. I blocked it with my left forearm, which hurt far more than I'd expected, and then drove a right into his thick chest. He stumbled back and I moved after him, trying to ignore the pain in both of my arms.

A middle-aged man wearing a black, unbuttoned vest and a white tieless shirt stepped out of a produce store and asked, "What's going on here?" I hit the taller man in the stomach with my left hand. His breath exploded from him and he doubled over and the man who'd come out of the produce store said, "Let's break it up." I kicked the tall man in the face, just as if I were trying for a sixty-yard punt. That straightened him up long enough so that the man in the white shirt and I could note how I'd ruined his looks. The beaked nose was smashed almost flat and some bone showed through the blood.

A small crowd had formed and a fat man in a blue suit asked the man in the vest and the white shirt what had happened. The man in the white shirt pointed at me and said, "That big guy's been beating up on these two little guys." Both of the little guys were an inch or so over six feet.

"Anybody call the cops?" the fat man asked.

"Nah. It's just getting started good."

The taller man with the ruined nose was now kneeling on the sidewalk, not too far from his friend with the bad kneecap, which I hoped would give him trouble for years to come. I picked up my attaché case and walked over to them. The tall man didn't know I was there. He didn't seem to know much of anything other than that his nose was a bloody, shapeless lump of pain. The shorter man, still sitting on the sidewalk, still holding his knee-cap, had stopped yelling. He looked up at me. I had some questions to ask him but I had to wait until he got tired of calling me five different kinds of moth-erfucker. Then I started to ask who had put him on to me, but I saw the blue uniform on the motor scooter down the street, so I turned and headed the other way—or started to. The fat man in the blue suit moved in front of me.

"You want something, friend?" I said.

"Those two guys are hurt real bad. You can't just—"

I put my hand on his chest and pressed gently. He didn't move. Instead, he stared at me with mean little blue eyes that were only slits in the fat folds of his face. "Those two guys are wanted in six states," I said. "If you hustle, you can nail 'em and beat the cops to the reward."

"How much reward?" he said.

"Six thousand in Pittsburgh and seventy-five hundred in Altoona. Bank jobs."

The fat man looked at me and then over my shoulder. He gave me another quick glance, as if hoping that there was something in my face that would let him believe me. Apparently there was because he stepped aside and I started across First Avenue. I'd only gone a few steps when there was a yell. I turned. The fat man stood over the dark Spanish-looking man whose nose I'd ruined. The dark man still knelt on the sidewalk and the fat man had an arm around his neck. He was choking him. At the same time he was trying to kick the smaller, blond man in the head. He missed in what must have been his second try, but the blond man yelled anyway and tried to crawl toward the curb. It hurt him to crawl and he yelled again as the fat man aimed another kick at his head, but again missed. The crowd was watching it all happen when the policeman arrived and I turned the corner.

The address on Avenue A that Padillo had given me was in a grimy seven-story apartment building which was located across the street from a dusty-looking park. It was a block of small, sour businesses that looked as if they could provide their owners a bare living, if the owners didn't eat too much and too often. There were two candy stores, a dry cleaner's, a small grocery, and a liquor store. None of them looked solvent and the liquor store for some reason appeared to be on the verge of bankruptcy. It may have been because of the defeated look in the eyes of its owner as he stood in the doorway, searching for whatever signs of Spring he could find in the dusty park across the street.

I glanced around before ducking through the dirty glass entrance door of the apartment house. No one on the street seemed interested in me. Not the dark young woman with the baby stroller that was stacked with old newspapers. Not the old man in the limp gray suit who used a cane to help him edge along the sidewalk. The liquor store owner had looked at me once, as if recognizing someone who could turn into an excellent customer. But he also seemed to know that I was a stranger in the neighborhood, the kind who would buy his liquor farther uptown.

The elevator in the tiled vestibule was large enough to carry two persons if one of them held his breath. I got in and studied the ancient controls and pushed enough buttons and slammed enough doors until the elevator finally gave a moan and grunt and started up to the seventh floor. It seemed like a long trip.

I was looking for 7-C and it was at the end of a hall, guarded by a sturdy wooden door that had a sheet of heavy-gauge steel bolted onto it, a decorative touch peculiar to New York. I knocked and glanced at my watch. It was five minutes past seven. Before

I could knock again, there was the sound of a bolt being drawn back and of some sturdy locks being disengaged. The door opened three inches and Padillo looked at me over the chain of the final lock.

"The plumber couldn't make it," I said.

"Jesus," he said and closed the door to undo the chain. He opened it and I went in and found myself in the living room of someone who was crazy about maple. A few of the pieces were new, but most of them were old, at least a hundred years or so, and all of them were maple and looked as if they were waxed every other day whether they needed it or not. What wasn't maple was giddy chintz if it were on a chair or a sofa or partially covering the windows. On the floor was hooked wool. It was all very quaint and just escaped being comfortable.

"Plomondon said no," Padillo said.

"He said he wasn't good enough anymore. Not good enough for Gitner anyway. He also said that he hopes you are."

"What are you puffing about? Doesn't the elevator work?"

"You can put the gun away," I said.

Padillo looked down at his right hand which was holding an automatic, a foreign make that I didn't recognize. He stuck it in his waistband, a little to the left of his navel. It had always seemed like an uncomfortable spot to me, but he liked it and I had seen it jump into his hand from there in less than four-tenths of a second, so I no longer felt qualified to comment on its inconvenience.

"I'm puffing, if you want to call it that, because I ran into a couple of guys down the street who wanted to beat up on me."

"Was it impulse or did they know you?"

"They knew who I was. They picked me up in Washington at the airport. I thought I'd lost them, but they're either smarter than I thought or I'm not as clever as well-meaning friends have led me to believe."

"Probably the latter," Padillo said. "If you were even half smart, you wouldn't be here. You'd be holding down your regular spot at the far end of the bar."

"Now that you've brought it up—"

"Scotch or bourbon?"

"Scotch."

Padillo disappeared into the kitchen that was just off the living room. I looked around some more. There were two closed doors and an open one that led to the bath. I assumed that the flat had two bedrooms. Padillo came back with the drinks and handed me one.

"Where's the king and the royal adviser?" I said.

He nodded toward one of the closed doors. "In there. It's got a one-inch iron bar across the door plus three other kinds of locks."

"Who lives here?"

"A forty-year-old spinster who's determined to maintain her virginity," Padillo said. "She's in Europe for a month or two. Wanda arranged for the place. I think the spinster is a distant cousin or something."

"Well, now that I'm here, what do you want me to do?"

"Go home."

"I thought you needed a fair hand."

"I need a pro, not an amateur. Not even a gifted one."

"Offer me money and I can leave the amateur ranks."

"Look at you," he said, shaking his head.

"That's little hard to do without a mirror."

"You're ten pounds overweight and most of it's in your gut. You should've got glasses three years ago but you're afraid that they'll spoil your aquiline profile. You think hard exercise is the five blocks that you walk home each night if the weather's just right. You're up to nearly three packs a day, you've got a cough that sounds like the second cousin to emphysema, and if the booze hasn't given you a hobnailed liver, it's not because you didn't go out for it. You're a mess."

"You forgot to mention my gums," I said. "I'm having a little trouble with them, too."

Padillo took a swallow of his drink. "What would you do with Amos Gitner?" he said. "He's faster than I am and I doubt that he's ever felt compunction and probably doesn't even know what the word means. I'm not going to be the one who tells Fredl that it all happened so fast that you couldn't possibly have suffered."

"I could sit on him," I said. "Squash him flat."

"There's that."

"Well, you need somebody and there aren't many that you can call on anymore, are there?"

He shook his head. "Not many. There never were really and most of them are dead now."

"Or scared."

"Not scared," he said. "Just sensible. That's something that no one could ever accuse you of."

"Do I go or stay?" I said. "You call it."

Padillo's dark Spanish eyes appraised me for several moments and then he shook his head again, a little sadly, I thought, as if only sentiment prevented him from dispatching the faithful old spaniel now that is teeth were gone. "Well, Christ," he said, "since you're already here."

"You don't know what this chance means to me."

"If it presents the opportunity to turn coward, take it."

"Your advice was always sound, if a little self-righteous."

"Cheap though," Padillo said, put his drink down, and turned toward one of the closed doors. "You might as well meet the king."

"What do I call him, King, your Excellency, or just Peter Paul?"

"Try Mr. Kassim, if 'you' doesn't seem to fit. He's supposed to be incognito."

"How does he like being king?"

"If we can keep him alive, he may like it just fine."

Chapter 11

The king came out first. I didn't think that he looked much like a king, but that's another field in which my expertise is limited. He shook hands with me after Padillo introduced him as Mr. Kassim which I thought was a nice egalitarian touch. He said, "I am very pleased to make your acquaintance," pronouncing each word without accent, other than the kind that you would pick up from an English tutor. He spoke as if he hadn't used the language in quite a while and was trying it on again with some trepidation, like last summer's suit.

I was next introduced to Emory Scales, ex-tutor and now grand royal adviser to the Kingdom of Llaquah. He also shook hands with me and I felt that it was for the first and last time, but that's the way a lot of Englishmen shake hands and I no longer think much about it.

Scales was an elbow man, nearly always at Kassim's right one, almost nudging it, but not quite as he bent slightly forward, his long, skinny face constantly turning this way and that, depending on who was doing the talking, the king or someone else. Scales moved his lips a little when the king spoke, much like a ventriloquist and his dummy. I decided that he was a royal adviser who took his duties seriously.

They were an incongruous pair. The king himself was short, plump and totally bald at twenty-one. Either that or the monastery where he'd spent the last five years had a thing about shaved heads. His eyes jumped around almost constantly, as if seeking something comfortable and reassuring to look at and seldom finding it in other people's faces. He smiled a lot, too, but I put that down to nervousness since his teeth were bad and not very rewarding to look at. Now that he was almost rich I thought that he might afford an inexpensive cap job or at least a toothbrush.

Scales, even with his hovering posture, loomed over Kassim. If he had straightened up he would have been as tall as I and a lot slimmer. I judged him to be somewhere near fifty, a little seedy, a little worn, even a little sad. It may have been his first and last chance at the big time and he was afraid that he would muff it. But then I always read too much into things.

After we had shaken hands, Scales turned toward Padillo and said, "I thought that you said a Mr. Plomondon would be joining you."

"He couldn't make it so I persuaded Mr. McCorkle to accept the assignment." There was always that about Padillo—he lied beautifully.

"You are a very big man," Kassim said to me and let me have another look at his awful teeth.

I didn't see any reason to apologize for my size, only ten pounds of which could be blamed on self-indulgence, so I contented myself with an answering smile and a nod.

"The bigger they are," the king said carefully, "the harder they fall." He beamed when he got it all out and then turned to Scales and said, "Is that not correct, Mr. Scales?"

"It is the correct idiomatic expression, your Majesty, but scarcely appropriate for the occasion."

Kassim nodded his understanding and turned back to me. "I did not mean to offend, Mr. McCorkle. It is only that I have not spoken English in many years and I am trying to recall it. Have you had much experience in guardingbody?"

"Bodyguarding," Scales said, almost automatically, as if he'd been correcting Kassim for days.

The king didn't seem to mind. "Yes, bodyguarding," he said.

"Some," I said, "but not nearly as much as Mr. Padillo, of course."

"We may have to move from here ahead of schedule," Padillo said. "McCorkle ran into some trouble on his way up from Washington. It looks as if they know that we're here."

"Was it Kragstein and Gitner?" Scales asked me.

"No. I'd never seen this pair before. I thought I'd lost them uptown, but they seemed to know where I was heading."

"That means that they have added to their strength," Scales said.

"Maybe not," I said. "Those two won't trouble anyone for a while. They may even be in jail right now."

"Are you responsible for their—uh—misfortune, Mr. McCorkle?" Kassim said, putting a trace of real humor into his nervous smile.

"Partly, at least."

"Do you have an alternate place in mind, Mr. Padillo?" Scales said.

"Here in New York?"

"Yes."

"I can locate one if we need it. What we need

more than another hideout is that call from Wanda Gothar."

Scales fished an old-fashioned gold pocket watch from his vest and snapped it open. "It's nearly seven thirty," he said. "She should be calling any minute."

No one said anything for a while as though we all expected the phone to ring right on cue. When it didn't, Padillo said to me, "Wanda's been making the arrangements with the oil companies for Mr. Kassim to sign certain papers."

"Why don't they just send them over here by messenger?" I said. "We could probably find a notary down at the corner."

"I'm afraid that the magnitude of the transaction prevents that, Mr. McCorkle," Scales said. "Although the preliminary negotiations were conducted by his Majesty's late brother, there must—for a number of reasons, some political, some not—there must be a certain amount of formality and protocol, even grandeur, if you will, incorporated into the actual signing of the documents."

"You're not going to do it publicly, are you?" I said.

"No, but nevertheless there will be appropriate ceremony and this is to be recorded on film. The films will be shown throughout Llaquah as part of an educational program that will acquaint the people with the significance of the transaction."

"Will it be just Mr. Kassim by himself," I said, "or will other representatives of Llaquah attend?"

The king smiled nervously again and ran his right hand over his smooth head as if testing to see whether it needed another shave. "I'm afraid, Mr.

McCorkle, that the representatives of Llaquah who are in this country are also the employers of Messrs. Gitner and Kragstein. My fellow countrymen are not at all anxious for my Patrick Henry to appear on the documents. They would prefer their own signatures."

"John Henry, I believe," Scales murmured, looking at Padillo for confirmation.

"John Henry," Padillo said. "But whoever signs the documents gets the bonus which is four million dollars."

"Five million," Scales said. He said it almost dreamily, as if there really weren't that much money in the world. He was silent for a moment and he may have been counting his share of the prize again. "I suppose it must sound like a rather bizarre situation, but we live in unusual times and in this particular case, extremely high stakes are involved. For some, it is a matter of personal gain. For his Majesty, it is the opportunity to transform his country from a poverty-stricken desert waste into one of the economic wonders of the world in which all of the people—"

Scales might have gone on for another fifteen minutes if the phone hadn't rung. Padillo answered it with a curt hello and then began listening. I watched the knuckles of his right hand blanch as his grip tightened. He didn't say good-bye before he hung up and if he didn't slam the instrument down, neither did he use any gentleness when he recradled it. He turned toward us and his mouth was stretched into that thin, hard line that made his lips seem bloodless.

"Miss Gothar?" Scales asked.

Padillo shook his head. "No," he said. "Franz Kragstein."

"Dear me," Scales said, which must have meant that he was distressed. "What did he say?"

"He's giving us an hour."

"To do what?" Scales said.

"To get out of here."

"And if we don't?"

"He'll come in after us."

Kassim produced one of his nervous smiles. "But how could he possibly do that? Is not our door impregnated?"

"Impregnable," Scales said.

Padillo turned to give the door a look. "It's neither to Kragstein," he said.

"What is it then?" Scales said.

"To him it's just another door."

I didn't like the sound of it so I decided to say so. "It doesn't make sense."

"What?" Padillo said.

"Why should he call you? Why not just make his try?"

"Where would you rather try it, here or out on the street?"

"If I were Kragstein, out on the street."

"So it would be wiser to remain where we are?" Scales said, making it a question out of politeness. He seemed more worried about the king's occasional grammatical lapses than he did about Kragstein's threats. The king wasn't exactly quivering either. He had chosen a chintz-covered armchair and was leaning back in it, smiling at whoever paid him any attention, anxious to please, and eager to keep out of the way. If one had to be a bodyguard, the king seemed to be the perfect client.

"We stay here until Wanda calls," Padillo said. "Then we move."

"And you have a place in mind?" Scales asked.

"Only if we need it," Padillo said.

Conversation ended and we sat there in the maple- and chintz-furnished living room of the apartment that was located in what they used to call New York's teeming lower East Side and examined the hooked rugs on the floor and the pastoral prints on the walls and the thoughts that slid through our minds and then we jumped, almost in unison, when the phone rang. Padillo got it before it rang twice and after he said hello he nodded at us so that we would know that it was Wanda. He said, "Hold on," into the phone and gestured toward the room where the king and Scales had been when I arrived. "There's an extension in there," he said. "Get on it."

The phone was next to the bed and I picked it up and said nothing.

"McCorkle's on," Padillo said.

"Why?" Wanda Gothar said.

"Because he's in now. All the way."

"You said Plomondon."

"He thought Gitner was a little rich."

"And McCorkle doesn't?"

"He doesn't know Gitner that well."

"He can't handle Gitner," she said. "I'm not even sure that you can."

"We may get the chance to settle that question in about fifteen minutes. Kragstein wants us out of here by then or they're coming in."

"Take care of it," she said. She had no questions, no comments, not even any advice. Just the automatic admonition which assumed that Padillo would know how to do it just like he'd know how to pick up a quart of ice cream on the way home from work.

"How long have we got in New York?" he said.

"Two more days."

"Then?"

"San Francisco."

"That's not just dumb," he said "that's inexcusable."

"The oil companies don't need any excuse," she said. "That's where the signing takes place. They won't change it. I tried."

"Why don't you quote them the odds against us making a cross-country trip like that with the opposition we've got."

"I did," she said. "They seemed delighted."

"You mean they don't want the deal?"

"They'll take it, but if something happened to Kassim, they think they could make another one that could be even better."

"All right," Padillo said. "I'll give you a number where you can get me for the next two days." He rattled one off without hesitation and I was fairly certain that Wanda Gothar didn't need to write it down. They both had memories like that—the kind that could recall the combinations on their high school lockers.

"I'll call you from San Francisco," she said.

"Where are you now?"

"Where the power is," she said. "Dallas."

"Call me this time tomorrow."

"All right," she said. "By the way, Mr. McCorkle?"

"Yes?" I said.

"Shall I be seeing you in San Francisco?"

"Perhaps," I said.

"It's such a beautiful city. Do you like it?"

"My opinion doesn't count much. I was born there."

"Really? Then I hope you're not planning to die there."

She broke the connection before I could say something that would show off my incisive wit so I hung up the phone and spent a few moments admiring the spinister's bedroom. It was really a boudoir in the classic French sense of the word which meant that it was a place to sulk in if the diamonds in the bracelet weren't big enough or if the monthly check was a couple of days late. Although the living room might be chintz and maple, the bedroom was all sex and sin with lots of mirrors and a big round bed with a fur spread that looked like seal, but could have been sable, and careful lighting and a chaise lounge big enough for two in case the bed got boring. It could have been the bedroom of a top-dollar call girl, or of a spinster who yearned to be one. Either way I had to feel sorry for her.

When I came out of the bedroom the first thing I saw was the king as he knelt by his chair, his hands clasped in front of him, his head up, his eyes closed, and his lips moving silently, presumably in prayer. Scales was watching him with what I took to be benign approval and Padillo, a failed Catholic of sorts himself, was checking the action on his automatic and looking as though he didn't have too much faith in that either.

I stood there in the doorway of the bedroom for a while, shifting from one foot to the other until the king got through with his prayers. He signaled their conclusion by saying "Amen" aloud in a ringing, fervent voice and Padillo looked up at me and said, "Did you bring anything to shoot with?"

"The office thirty-eight," I said and wondered if it were a good time to tell him that I'd forgotten to pack the bullets. Either he was a mind reader or he was resigned to my careless ways because he reached into his coat pocket and tossed me a box of .38 shells. "In case you run short," he said and I thought that he should get some sort of prize for tact.

I took the revolver out of the attaché case and loaded it and then dropped it into the right-hand pocket of my jacket so that it was sure to ruin the drape. Padillo rose from his chair and crossed to a window and peered out through the cheery patterned drapes that were dyed rust and lemon and what looked for all the world like British Racing Green. Padillo looked through the drapes for a moment and then turned, crossed to the phone, and dialed a number.

"It's Padillo," he said and then listened for almost a minute, his eyes squeezed shut as he massaged the bridge of his nose.

When he said, 'I've been awfully tied up down in Washington," I knew it was a woman because it was the same thing that he told women in Washington, except that when he was there he was always being tied up in New York.

"Some friends of mine are in town and we need a place to stay for a couple of days," he said, "No," he said, "all men." There was another pause while he listened and massaged his nose some more and then he said, "No, I don't want you to go to all that trouble... Yes, I know that's what you pay them for." He looked at his watch and said, "We should be there within an hour . . . All right . . . Thanks very much."

He hung up the phone and then looked at us, one at a time, as if trying to decide whether we were really worth some private sacrifice that he had to make. "It's a cooperative apartment in the Sixties just off Fifth," he said. "All we've got to do is get there."

"I don't mean to carp, Mr. Padillo," Scales said, "but won't another apartment be just as vulnerable as this one?"

"It's not exactly an apartment," Padillo said. "It's the entire floor of a building and the person who owns it has something that makes it secure enough for the Secret Service to give it a top rating."

"What does this person have?" Kassim said.

"The best protection there is," Padillo said. "About eighty million dollars."

Chapter 12

It was dark on the roof of the apartment building, but seven stories below a street lamp flooded the entrance with a pool of yellow light that had a sickly, jaundiced look about it. I peered over the three-foot-high brick wall that ran along the front of the building. The king and Emory Scales knelt beside me, but they weren't looking down. They were looking to their left at the eight-foot-wide black void that they were going to have to leap across in about three minutes if Padillo's plan worked.

Eight feet is a very long way to jump if you're a little plump and a little out of shape, like the king, or over fifty with the coordination not what it once was, like Emory Scales, or a sedentary creature of slothful habits whose conception of giddy height is a four-foot bar stool—like me.

It was a typical Padillo plan, devoid of frippery, stark in its simplicity, and commendable for its cunning, but if no one seemed much inclined to talk about its risk, that was understandable, too. I wasn't quite sure that the danger was evenly distributed. Kassim, Scales and I had to summon up some heretofore untapped and probably nonexistent reserves of nerve and strength to leap a chasm that would have given pause to a mountain goat. All Padillo had to do was get shot at.

There was only a scattering of pedestrians on the

sidewalk and traffic on Avenue A was light. Across the street the park looked ominous and forbidding, the way most city parks look now when the sun goes down.

A light blue two-door, the kind that they used to call a club coupe, rolled slowly down Avenue A from the left. It was one of those cars that have big engines, anywhere from 350 to 425 cubic inches, and are named after some reptile or fish, and are just the thing for heavy city traffic if you need the reassurance of a speedometer that goes all the way up to 160 miles per hour.

The car came slowly down the avenue as if its driver was looking for either a place to park or a girl to pick up. It was going to be a matter of timing and luck. "If he's sober," Padillo had said, "and if he's got normal reactions and if he's not daydreaming, it should work out okay."

"That doesn't leave much room for improvisation," I'd said.

"Not much at all," Padillo had said.

The car was about forty feet from the entrance of the apartment building and I judged its speed to be around twenty miles per hour. A dark figure, moving almost too fast to be human, darted into the street lamp's pool of yellow light for less than a second, and then he was in the street directly in the path of the oncoming car. The driver was awake. He slammed on his brakes and the wheels grabbed at the asphalt and the front end dipped until the heavy chrome bumper was almost at the level of the man's ankles.

The man was momentarily caught in the car's lights, fully illuminated, unable to move until he was sure the car could stop without striking him. It must have been much less than a second, but it was long enough for whoever was in the park across the street to get off two shots, but by then Padillo was moving again, ducking low, as he scuttled around to the right-hand side of the car and jerked at its handle. The door was locked and the driver was starting off again slowly, apparently not yet quite sure what was happening, only that he wanted no part of it. Padillo smashed the right window with his automatic and I could see the driver's hand come over and raise the catch. Then Padillo was inside and the car was frantically spinning its rear wheels when I said, "Let's go," to Kassim and Scales.

I heard two more shots, apparently from the park, but I didn't look. Instead, I backed up twenty feet, paused and started my run. The eight feet of blackness that separated the two buildings assumed Olympic proportions and I kept trying to remember to take off with my right foot but by the time I got to the edge of the building it was too late and I had to use my left one and then I was in the air for a couple of hours and finally landed hard on the gritty roof with a good six feet to spare.

I turned and hurried back to the edge of the building, ready to grab for Kassim or Scales if their feet slipped and they started to teeter on the edge after they landed. There was just enough light so that I could make them out. But neither of them was down in a sprinter's crouch. They were standing and one of them was whimpering. It was the king. He didn't want to try the leap and he was telling Scales why in English, and when he got tired of that, in French. I saw Scales's right arm go back and then the figures blurred together. But if I couldn't see it, I could hear it all right. It was the sound of a hard slap and I wondered who was the more surprised, the king who got slapped or the royal adviser who delivered the blow.

The whimpering suddenly stopped and then a short, dumpy figure was trotting slowly across the opposite roof toward me, lumbering really, and I didn't see how he could make it, but he picked up a little speed and then sailed off into the night, his arms and legs frantically in motion as if he were still running. Kassim landed heavily only six inches from the edge of the building and I caught his left arm just before his feet went out from under him. I dragged him a couple of feet and then let him go. He started whimpering again.

I turned and watched Scales. He ran all right but when he reached the edge of the building he got his feet confused and couldn't decide which one he should use to give him the lift and by the time he got that straightened out it was too late. But he was in the air by then, flapping his arms as if he had decided to fly the rest of the way. He landed hard, with his elbows clutching the ledge of the building as he scrabbled for a hold. I caught him and pulled him up and over and then let him lie there for a moment.

I ran to the front of the building we'd jumped to and looked down at the street. A man had come out of the park and was running across the street toward the building we had just left. He ran easily and there was a nice spring to his step. Even at night from seven floors up I had no trouble recognizing Amos Gitner.

I hurried back to Kassim and Scales. The king had stopped whimpering, but he looked a little ashamed of himself and smiled at me nervously, as if he hoped that I'd have something complimentary to say about how nicely he had jumped. Instead I said, "Gitner's on his way."

That got Scales up off the roof where he'd sat picking at the torn elbow of his shiny blue suit. "It's torn," he said.

"When the king gets all the money, maybe he'll buy you a new one. Let's go."

Scales turned toward Kassim. "I apologize for having struck you, your Majesty, but given the circumstances—" He didn't finish the sentence, perhaps because there was nothing in his background and training that would provide him with an excuse for having struck a royal person. "You jumped very well," he said in a lame tone.

Kassim brightened. "Thank you, Scales."

"Let's go," I said again.

We moved over rooftops until we came to the building that formed the corner on Avenue A and Ninth Street. We started down the fire escape. At the second floor, I climbed on the ladder that screeched and howled as it slid slowly toward the sidewalk. The king and Scales followed.

I started trotting up Ninth, herding Scales and the king ahead of me. We cut left on First Avenue and then started walking rapidly up St. Mark's Place, past the Polish Democratic Club and the Scorpiana Boutique, walking as quickly as we could toward Astor Place and Cooper Square.

I kept looking back but he didn't show himself until we had nearly reached the square. Gitner was running toward us. He ran fast and I snapped, "Go!" at the king and Scales and they fairly bounded down the steps of the subway entrance, as if trying to compensate for their twin flops in the running broad jump event.

Gitner was just crossing the street as I jumped down the first three steps of the subway stairs. I dropped the tokens that Padillo had given me into the turnstile and shoved the king and Scales through. Then there was nothing to do but wait for the next train.

I heard it coming, and it seemed a long way off, but then it was there and we darted into it. I turned to watch the turnstiles. Gitner was racing toward them now and he had his token ready. He would. Then he was through the turnstile and running for the train as the doors began to close, ever so slowly. Gitner was at the doors, clawing at them now, but they had closed, and we stood there and stared at each other until the train began to move.

Neither of us waved good-bye.

It was on Sixty-fourth Street, a little east of Fifth Avenue, twenty stories or so of dark beige brick that had accumulated its fair share of the city's soot and grime. There was not much to set it apart from other New York apartment buildings that had gone up in the late twenties or early thirties, not unless you counted the steel bars that had been twisted and painted to make them look like wrought iron. There probably wasn't a second-story man alive who stood a chance against the bars and just to make sure the management had covered every window with them all the way up to the fourth floor.

The doorman was a little different, too, because there were three of them and they were far too young for their jobs, somewhere in their mid-twenties, and they seemed to do everything as a team, even opening the front door. One of them would actually do the work and the other two would stand back, one of them watching the street and the other watching whoever went in or came out. The ones who watched kept their right hands in the deep pockets of their long blue uniform coats that the tailor had done such a good job with that unless you looked closely you could scarcely tell that there was something else in the pockets besides hands. I guessed them to be small-caliber automatics, no larger than a .32, but I might have been wrong. They could just as easily have been .25's.

It was the third taxi we'd taken since leaving the subway at Grand Central and when it rolled up in front of the apartment entrance, number one opened the door for us, number two quartered the street to make sure that nobody shot at us, and number three stood back and away, poised and ready, just in case we tried something funny.

"Mr. McCorkle?" said the one who'd opened the door.

"That's me," I said and bent down to pay off the driver.

"Mr. Padillo is waiting for you in the lobby."

"Thank you."

The one who'd spoken also opened the door to the apartment and the king went first, then Scales, and I was almost last, but not quite, because the two other doormen were right behind me and they stayed there until they saw Padillo nod twice.

He stood in the center of what I suppose could be called the lobby although it contained no chairs or couches or settees, not even a potted plant. But there were about seventy-five thousand dollars' worth of Oriental rugs on the floor and four or five paintings on the walls that rightfully should have been in the Metropolitan, and there was also a desk. It was a plain walnut desk of contemporary design and just below its waxed, uncluttered top were six holes that could have been decorative, but which I also noted were large enough to launch tear gas shells. I didn't even bother to look for the closed-circuit television cameras.

There were two men behind the desk and they half rose when we came in, but kept their hands out of sight underneath the desk, probably on some trigger or other that could blow us all up. I'd once had occasion to go calling on a Vice-President in his office on the Senate side of the Capitol and there had been two men there who had risen in just that same way—attentive and polite, but so tightly coiled that I had the feeling that if I'd raised an eyebrow the wrong way they might have blown my head off. After the Kennedys and King, I couldn't much blame them.

When the two men saw that Padillo recognized us, they settled back down behind the desk. But they watched us. My back was to them, but I didn't have to turn to know that they were watching. I could feel it.

"You have any trouble?" Padillo said, motioning to the bank of elevators.

"Not much," I said. "It was nearly a tie at the subway, but Gitner was five seconds late."

"I figured that he'd be two minutes behind you," Padillo said. "He must have learned a few things."

"What about yourself?" I said.

"Kragstein followed me. I didn't have time to lose him so he knows that we're here."

"What happened to the guy whose car you stopped?"

"I gave him a hundred which made him so happy that he wanted to know if I'd like to do it again next week. He's out of a job and blames it all on Neville Chamberlain and Munich. I couldn't quite follow his reasoning."

Kassim turned from his inspection of the lobby and said, "Do you consider this building to be adequately secure, Mr. Padillo?"

"It's been favorably compared with Fort Knox—and with reason."

The elevator arrived then and I saw the validity in Padillo's claim. It was the only elevator I ever rode that had a copilot.

They let us off on the nineteenth floor where a man waited for us in a small, richly furnished room that faced the elevator. The man had curly gray hair and wore a dark, almost black suit and a deferential maner. "Good evening, Mr. Padillo," he said and there was a trace of the South in his voice. "Dinner will be ready shortly, but Mrs. Clarkmann thought that you might like to freshen up first."

"Thank you, William," Padillo said. He turned to the king and Scales. "Mr. Kassim and Mr. Scales would probably like to. Also, Mr. Scales has torn his coat. Could you do something about it?"

"I'm sure I can, sir."

"Thank you. Mr. McCorkle and I will be at the bar. I know the way."

"Of course, sir," William said and turned to Kassim and Scales. "This way, gentlemen."

He led them through a door at the left. Padillo and I went straight ahead, through another door, and down a hall that was big enough to successfully carry off the two-foot-square black and white marble tiles that covered its floor and the three huge chandeliers that hung from its ceiling and cast their glittering light on the Louis Quatorze chairs and lowboys that lined the walls on either side and which didn't look as if they had been used for anything but decorative purposes for the past three hundred years.

"Is that Clarkmann with two n's?" I said.

"Right."

"Piston rings."

"Right again."

"Mr. Clarkmann died three years ago."

"You keep up with things."

"He left it all to her."

"Everything."

"She had a little to put in the pot herself, as I recall."

"About twenty million or so."

"Amanda Kent—the Kandy Kid, as a tabloid or two would have it."

"Kent's Candies, Incorporated," Padillo said. "Her grandfather founded it in Chicago and his major contribution was in refusing to spell candy with a K. A wise old bird."

We went through another door and into a room which was just what Padillo had said it would be, a bar. It was a dim place with all the bottles that one would need and an old bar that could have been rescued from a turn-of-the-century Third Avenue saloon. There were also some padded stools and some low tables surrounded by comfortable-looking leather chairs. It was a room designed for drinking and Padillo went behind the bar as if he knew the way.

"Scotch," I said and he poured us both doubles and after I'd tasted mine I admired the room some more and then waved my drink at it a little. "I don't like to be crass, but how much down would I have to have before I could move in?"

"As I said, it's a cooperative."

"Sort of a people's movement, huh?"

"You buy shares. One share equals one floor. One floor goes for one million."

"Isn't there what they call a maintenance charge?"

"I think it's twenty thousand a month, but I may be low."

"I won't haggle," I said. "Of course, I'd have to spend a little to furnish it."

"Another million, if you like nice things. By scrimping, you could get by for maybe seven hundred and fifty thousand."

"It's a long way from Santa Monica Boulevard," I said.

Padillo glanced around the room. "Too far?"

"Not with your charm."

"I met her at a party."

"You must know her pretty well if you can dump three unexpected weekend guests on her."

"I know her pretty well," he said.

"Is it serious?"

"It pleases her to think so and I like to please her."

I tasted my Scotch again. It was expensive stuff, too expensive for me even at wholesale prices. I waved my glass around again, but gently so as not to spill any. "There probably would be a tense period of adjustment, but I think I just might be able to get used to all this. A matter of self-discipline, I suppose."

Padillo grinned, but it was the wry kind that contained more regret than humor. "You'd last six months," he said. "Maybe a year."

"And you?"

"I think I'm afraid to find out."

"Maybe," I said, giving the room another look, "but I can see why you've spent so many weekends in New York. You use to hate it."

"There's that keen insight of yours again."

"Not really."

"What would you call it?"

I sighed and finished my drink. "Envy," I said. "The green kind."

Chapter 13

Even if her father and grandfather hadn't supplied half of the nation's chocolate bars, I could still see why the papers might have tagged her as the Kandy Kid. She had taffy-colored hair and cinnamon eyes and a creamy nougat complexion and a voice that was as smooth and as rich as melted butterscotch.

She was also a little over thirty, but with eighty million dollars you don't have to look it and she didn't. She came through the door to the bar, wearing something off-white that everyone would be wearing two or three years from then, and held out her hand and said, "I'm Amanda Clarkmann; you must be the McCorkle that he keeps talking about." She shook hands with me, a nice, firm friendly shake, and then she turned and kissed Padillo and it was a long, unabashed kiss which I watched and discovered what must have been a trace of voyeurism that I didn't know existed.

When it was over, Padillo said to me, "I've mentioned you a couple of times in passing."

"I can see why you changed your mind about New York."

"I've been trying to convince him that he should marry me for my money," she said. "Or sex. Even love."

"Offer to pay off his debts," I said.

"Does he owe much?"

I nodded. "He's in to me for nine bucks and our

head bartender told me to remind him of the five he borrowed last month when he needed cab fare."

"Bankruptcy—or the threat of it—has been known to make men do strange things," Padillo said. "Some commit suicide. Some try the South Seas. Some even get married." He mixed Amanda Clarkmann a drink and handed it to her.

"Tell me about his women," she said, smiling a little to let me know it was a joke, but not one funny enough to keep her from listening if I had something juicy to reveal.

"What can I say? Some were short and some were tall. The rest were kind of in between."

"How many?" she said, once more smiling, as if she hoped that the smile would erase the interest in her voice, but it didn't. She really wanted to know. Most women do.

"Ask him," I said.

"He won't talk about them."

"Then compliment him on his reticence."

"Were there many?"

"Women?"

"Yes."

"I never noticed a surplus," I said, "but neither was there a shortage. When it came to women, he always maintained what they used to call an ever-normal granary."

"If you have to talk about me," Padillo said, "would you try the present tense? The past tense gives me a perspective that I don't much care for."

"So what brings you back to New York so soon, Michael?" she said. "Mr. McCorkle here looks most presentable, but William sighed when I asked about your other two friends. That means they're a little odd."

"One of them's a king," Padillo said.

"Does he work at it?"

"He hopes to."

"He's the king of what? I should be able to guess because there aren't too many of them around anymore."

"Of Llaquah," Padillo said.

"His brother just died, didn't he? He was a pleasant man. A little frivolous, but pleasant."

"You knew him?" Padillo said.

She nodded. "We met a couple of times. Once in Paris and once in Madrid, I think. I didn't know him well. What do you call the new king?"

"I call him Mr. Kassim."

"Wouldn't he prefer 'your Majesty' or 'your Highness'?"

"Scales calls him that," I said.

"And who is Mr. Scales?"

"The royal adviser," Padillo said. "He used to be Kassim's tutor."

"The royal adviser has a torn sleeve, according to William."

"He fell down," I said.

She looked at Padillo and then at me and then back at Padillo. "Well, I can't say that the rest of his royal entourage is overly elegant."

"I don't know," I said. "What it lacks in elegance it makes up for in quiet competence and dogged loyalty."

"There's something else about it, too," Padillo said.

"What?" she asked.

"It's cheap."

"And the king is poor?"

"Today, he's broke. Next week he may be the richest king in the world."

"Then I know what I'll do," she said.

"What?" Padillo said.

"I'll try to cheer him up. Most of the kings I've known have been awfully sad."

The dining room that we gathered in that Friday night must have been the one that was used for those small, intimate parties of not more than a dozen guests. I don't know what it was called, or even if it had a name. The staff may have just referred to it as "Auxiliary Dining Room number six." Or seven. Or even eight.

Nor do I know who worked out the protocol, but we sat at a large round table with Kassim on Amanda Clarkmann's right, Padillo on her left, with me next to the king and Scales next to Padillo. In this case, "next" meant about three feet away.

The king seemed to be interested in the world's nicer things. He inspected the silver carefully, either to make sure that it was sterling or that it was clean. He turned a plate over to read its maker's name and whoever it was seemed to satisfy him. For someone who had just spent five years in a monastery, Kassim appeared inordinately interested in secular stuff. I decided that he may have felt that he had missed out on a lot and was now trying to catch up.

There were two to serve, a middle-aged man whom I'd have liked to have hired for the saloon and a younger one who was nearly as good. I would have given the chef a job, too, if I'd thought that we could afford him. He had done something miraculous to the veal and when the older man skillfully spooned another portion onto my plate, as if he thought of gluttony as a virtue, I knew how easily I might be corrupted. It didn't bother me.

Amanda Clarkmann kept the conversation going with effortless ease, directing most of it at the king who responded in monosyllables between bites. If his table talk and manners lacked polish, there was nothing wrong with his appetite. Whenever his hostess tried to steer the conversation toward Llaquah, the king redirected it toward the food, praising the veal so lavishly that she felt constrained to force a third portion on him.

After dinner, the king and Scales excused themselves, pleading weariness. Amanda Clarkmann, Padillo and I had brandy in a drawing room whose main feature was a Thomas Eakins portrait that hung above the fireplace. Padillo and I were on our second brandy and Amanda was still on her first when William, whom I took to be the household's major domo, brought in a phone, plugged it in, and informed Padillo that he had a call.

"Is there another jack in this room?" Padillo said.

"Yes, sir, there is."

"Can you get another phone and plug it in?"

William nodded, made a swift exit, and was back shortly with another phone which he also plugged in.

"Get on it," Padillo said to me.

"Would you like me to leave?" Amanda Clarkmann said.

Padillo shook his head. "I'll be listening mostly, not talking."

We picked up the phones together and Padillo said hello. There was a short pause and then a voice said, "Is that you, Padillo?" I didn't have any trouble placing the tone or the accent. Both of them belonged to Franz Kragstein.

"Give it up, Michael," he said with what seemed to be a touch of regret in his voice. "It's hopeless."

"You haven't done too well so far, Franz," Padillo said. "You can't even keep a line on McCorkle."

"It is hard to get competent help these days, isn't it?"

"I wouldn't know."

"While amiable enough, Mr. McCorkle doesn't seem to be overly experienced."

"He's fairly bright though. Inexpensive, too."

"We would like to reopen negotiations."

"No."

"Really, Michael, I don't understand why—"

"You don't have to understand why. All you need to know is that you and Gitner will have to go through me. If you want to try it, fine."

"I was only trying to be sensible. I am really quite fond of you, Michael, in my own way. It's paternal, I suppose. That is why I wanted to give you this—oh, I suppose I should call it this last opportunity. And no recriminations, of course."

"Hang up, Franz."

"I see. Well, I did try."

"Sure you did."

"One final item, Michael."

"All right."

"It's such a very long way to San Francisco."

"I've been there before."

"I'm sorry, Michael, that you won't again."

There was a click as Kragstein hung up and when the dial tone came on it seemed to have a shrill, insistent note that I hadn't heard before. But that may well be how all the dial tones sound in New York.

Chapter 14

The king was going for a grand slam in spades when Padillo came in and went behind the bar to mix himself a drink. Trumps were all in and the king used a spare one to get back to the board so that he could finesse his jack of hearts through me, but Amanda Clarkmann nailed the jack with her queen and the king was down one and doubled. He took it hard.

We had been playing bridge for nearly two hours that morning for a cent a point and the king and Scales were nearly thirty-five dollars ahead, probably because I hadn't played in more than ten years and hoped that it would be another ten before I was talked into trying it again, even with a partner who played as well as Amanda Clarkmann.

On the next hand the bidding stopped when she went to four hearts which would be not only game, but also rubber. It made me dummy so after I laid down my hand, I joined Padillo at the bar. It was nearly noon and I had nothing to do until Wanda Gothar called that evening so I went behind the bar and mixed a martini, lying to myself as usual that it was needed to spark the appetite.

"Who's winning?" Padillo said as I debated about whether I wanted an olive.

"They are," I said, deciding that I didn't really need the extra calories.

"I ordered the armored truck."

"The armored truck," I said wisely and took a quick swallow of the martini.

"It's due at four."

"The banks will be closed by then," I said, once again demonstrating that I can keep up my end of any conversation.

"It's not going to a bank."

"Of course not."

"It's going to the airport."

"LaGuardia," I said, just to give him the chance to correct me. It made him feel better.

"Kennedy."

"Well, I've heard that they make them so that they're pretty comfortable nowadays."

"We won't be in it."

"This came to you in the night, I assume."

"Around two."

"As a diversionary measure," I said, "it has a touch of genius."

"It's half good and it gives us half a chance," he said, "which is about one hundred percent better than we had before."

"What's going to the airport? In the armored car, I mean."

"The ring."

"The good one, of course."

"Amanda says that it's insured for five hundred thousand."

"And where does the ring go once it gets to the airport?"

"To a jeweler in San Francisco. He'll clean it and send it back."

"But our nemeses, Mr. Kragstein and Mr. Gitner, will think that this is just a ruse—that we're really inside the armored truck."

"That's it."

"And while they're following or pursuing the armored truck, we'll be heading somewhere else."

"Newark," Padillo said.

"Ah, Newark."

"Then to Denver."

"Of course."

"And from Denver guess where."

"If I said San Francisco, I'd be wrong so I'll say Los Angeles."

"You're right."

"Where we rent a car and drive to San Francisco, sneaking in the back door so to speak. Whose armored truck is it, Brink's?"

"It's the other outfit," he said, "the one with the red ones."

"I've never ordered an armored truck," I said, "probably because I felt that they'd be picky about having me as a customer. Did they give you any static?"

"I doubt that they'd give me the time. But then my Dun and Bradstreet rating doesn't glow in the dark the way Amanda's does."

"She ordered it," I said.

Padillo nodded.

"I can't think of any disadvantages in being rich," I said.

Padillo looked around the room. "Only one," he said.

"What?"

"Worrying that someday you might be poor."

After the game broke up and Amanda and I paid the king and Scales the $31.58 that we owed them, she excused herself, and the older of the two men who had waited on us the night before served lunch in the same room where we had played bridge.

Lunch was a shrimp cocktail with a sauce whose recipe I would have paid $100 for, thick rare roast beef sandwiches, and a Mexican beer that I'd never tried before but liked very much. The king said he didn't drink beer, so he was brought a Coca-Cola.

During lunch Padillo told the king and Scales about the armored truck. They exchanged glances and after the king caught Scale's almost imperceptible nod, he beamed and complimented Padillo on his deviation.

"I think you mean deviousness, your Majesty," Scales murmured, looking a little embarrassed. The king beamed happily and said yes, that's what he had meant all along. "It will also give me the opportunity to see more of your great country than I had thought possible," he said, making it sound as though he felt that Padillo and I ranked not too far below the President and considerably above the Secretary of State.

Just before the coffee was served, the king got another one of those almost invisible nods from Scales. He rose, smoothing his bald head again, and begged to be excused, mentioning that it was time for his afternoon meditations.

When he was gone, Scales leaned across the table toward us in a confidential if not conspiratorial manner, said "uh" a couple of times, and then asked, "I had no wish to alarm his Majesty, of course, but are you quite convinced that this is our safest route to San Francisco?"

"There aren't any safe routes," Padillo said. "But this is the best I can come up with unless you change your mind about bringing in either the local cops or the Secret Service. I'd recommend both."

Scales frowned, shook his head twice, and said, "Impossible," in a tone that clearly implied that further discussion would be unwelcome.

It didn't bother Padillo. "Why?" he said.

Scales pulled at the end of his long, skinny nose, looking first at Padillo and then at me, as if trying to decide whether we could be trusted with some more royal secrets. "I haven't brought this up before because you might think it a bit ridiculous," he said.

"Try us," Padillo said.

"His Majesty—this is not critical, mind you—but his Majesty has a theory that amounts almost to an obsession."

"About what?"

"Your Secret Service. He blames them, you know."

"For what?"

"For the death of President Kennedy. Also his brother's. His Majesty is convinced that it was a gigantic conspiracy and that the Secret Service was in the thick of it."

"That's not only dumb, it's ridiculous," Padillo said.

"The Secret Service wasn't even assigned to Robert Kennedy," I said.

"His Majesty's point exactly," Scales said. "'Why not?' he asks. Mind you, he's read virtually everything that has been written on the subject and he is totally convinced of this conspiracy theory. It's become an obsession with him and that's why he's so adamant about refusing Secret Service protection. He is positive that they can be suborned."

A look of tired disgust crept over Padillo's face. "All right," he said. "The Secret Service is on the take. What about the local police?"

Scales ran a finger around the inside of his collar, straining his neck this way and that. His pale face grew a trifle pink. "Doctor King," he murmured. "And Dallas."

"The local cops are crooked, too," Padillo said, nodding his head slightly and biting his lower lip to keep from either laughing or screaming.

"Of this, his Majesty is convinced."

"What about the Gothars?" Padillo said. "What about McCorkle and me?"

"The Gothars had impeccable credentials, but just to make certain I had them doublechecked—at no small expense, I might add."

"Who recommended me?" Padillo said. "As I understand it, the Gothars had to make me part of their package."

"That is entirely correct," Scales said. "You have an admirer who once was in British Intelligence, Mr. Padillo. I leaned heavily upon him for advice. He recommended the Gothars as well as you."

"What's his name?"

"He prefers to remain anonymous and I respect his wishes."

"You should have spent some of that money checking out Kragstein and Gitner," Padillo said. "Then you might have frightened Kassim into agreeing to Secret Service protection."

"His Majesty is well aware of their reputation," Scales said, a little stiffly. "That's why your services were engaged."

"Because I'm supposed to be better than Gitner?"

Scales smiled for the first time in what must have

been a long while. "Not better, Mr. Padillo," he said. "But more honest. Decidedly more honest."

I was back in the room that contained the bar at three thirty that afternoon. After Scales left us, Padillo and I had talked in a desultory manner for twenty minutes or so and then he had gone in search of Amanda Clarkmann to thank her for her hospitality or to say good-bye or to accept her offer of marriage. I never did find out which.

I did find another bottle of the Mexican beer and took it back to my room and sipped it while I read a new novel that a lot of critics had liked about a youngster from the Midwest who was trying to make up his mind whether to go to Canada or Vietnam. When he chose Canada, I gave a small cheer, put the book down, and headed for the room that contained the bar. Padillo and Amanda Clarkmann came in a few minutes later and since both of them seemed to be glowing more than usual I assumed that they had spent a pleasant enough afternoon together, probably in bed.

The king and Scales joined us and then William, the major domo, wheeled in some coffee along with the information that Amanda was wanted on the phone. She used the one near the bar and when she rejoined us she said, "That was the armored truck company. They're going to be fifteen minutes early. I told William to notify the security people downstairs."

Padillo looked at his watch. "We have time for one cup, I think."

Amanda Clarkmann poured and served the coffee and offered around a place of nice little sandwiches, but no one took any except the king, who took four.

After we walked down the wide hall with the chandeliers, the black and white marble floor, and the Louis Quatorze furniture. Amanda Clarkmann carried a small gray velvet box that I assumed contained the ring. I wouldn't have minded a look at a ring that was insured for half a million dollars, but I couldn't bring myself to ask.

At three forty-five we were all standing in the foyer that faced the elevators. Padillo was next to Amanda. I was between the king and Scales. There was a soft bong from a bell as the elevator reached the nineteenth floor and the doors opened and two men in gray uniforms with drawn guns stepped out into the foyer.

It had gone just like Padillo had planned it. The only thing wrong was that one of the men with a drawn gun and a gray uniform was Amos Gitner.

Chapter 15

Padillo was the one to take out first and Gitner knew it. He fired once, then twice, and there was a shrill scream, but Padillo was already halfway across the room in a low flat racing dive. He landed on his left shoulder, went into a roll, and when he came up his automatic was in his right hand. The other man in the gray uniform had stepped out into the foyer, blocking Gitner temporarily. For less than a second the man seemed to debate whether to shoot the king or Padillo. He chose Padillo, but I threw my attaché case at him with a hard underhand throw. The attaché case hit his right hand just as he fired. Padillo shot him twice in the chest and he stumbled back against Gitner.

I spun toward the king and Scales. The king was already turned and racing down the black and white marbled hall. He ran fast, much faster than he'd run on the rooftop. Scales was right behind him.

I turned back, clawing my revolver from my coat pocket in what must have been the slowest draw in Christendom. Padillo again fired twice as he moved, this time scuttling sideways. He shot the man he'd shot before, hitting him again in the chest, killing him probably. Gitner had his left arm around the man's waist now, holding him up, using him for a shield as he backed into the elevator where I could see the bodies of its two operators sprawled on the floor.

Gitner had to punch the elevator button with his right hand, the one that held his revolver. Then he fired once, twice, three times—spacing his shots, not trying to hit anything, just making sure that no one rushed the elevator until the doors closed. As they closed, Padillo jumped for the button, and mashed it, trying to make the doors reopen. He was either too late or the controls didn't work that way. Gitner was gone and Amanda Clarkmann lay dead against the wall below a quite good watercolor that showed a street scene of Paris in the Spring.

She had screamed only once, probably when Gitner's first bullet had struck her shoulder. The second one had gone into her throat and had made a mess of it. Padillo walked slowly across the room and looked down at her. I couldn't see the expression on his face. I didn't really want to.

When he turned he looked at me, almost curiously, and said, "He used a Magnum. A .357 Magnum. Did you notice that?" He didn't wait for an answer. Instead, he turned and walked down the marbled hall, his automatic dangling and forgotten in his right hand. I followed.

Once more in the room that contained the bar, Padillo picked up one of the phones and dialed ten numbers. He waited nearly a minute until someone said hello and then he said, "This is Padillo, Burmser. Amos Gitner just shot and killed Amanda Clarkmann in her New York apartment. I'm leaving for San Francisco with the king. Fix it." Then he hung up.

I had gone around the bar and poured two double Scotches. I handed him one and he drank it down slowly, not taking the glass from his lips until it was empty.

William burst into the room, his usually imperturbable face contorted into fear and horror and, I suppose, even rage. He stopped short when he saw the automatic in Padillo's right hand which he was still holding and had held, even when he'd dialed the phone.

Padillo looked at him. "Mrs. Clarkmann has been killed," he said in an almost toneless voice.

"I—I—I" William stopped to gulp down some air.

"Don't say anything," Padillo said. "Just listen. The police will be here shortly. But before they arrive, there'll be some men here from the Government. The Federal Government. They'll tell you what to do and what to say. Do you understand?"

It took him four tries to get it out, but finally William said, "Yes, sir."

"Now you need to do three things. Are you listening?"

"Yes, sir," William said, some calmer now, but not much.

"Get me the keys to Mrs. Clarkmann's Oldsmobile. That's one. Two, find Mr. Kassim and Mr. Scales and tell them to meet me here. Three, cover up Mrs. Clarkmann. Use a blanket."

This time William only nodded before he hurried away, but his face had lost some of its tortured look. He seemed almost glad that there was someone around to tell him what to do.

Padillo turned back toward me and then looked down at his hands which were holding the empty glass and the automatic. He handed the glass to me and stuck the gun back in the waistband of his trousers.

"You want another one?" I said, gesturing with the glass.

He nodded, not looking at me, not looking really at anything.

"They must have tapped into the central panel box," he said, more to himself than to me.

I handed him his drink. "I thought that was a tough job, especially in this building."

Padillo shook his head. "Not for Kragstein. He'd have someone legitimate from the phone company do it. It wouldn't cost him anything. He'd blackmail them into it. He works that way, not because he has to but because he likes to."

"That's how they knew about the armored truck."

"That's how."

"Do you think they hijacked it?"

"God knows," Padillo said. "Maybe they rented one and then called Amanda and told her that they'd be fifteen minutes early. You can rent anything you want in New York if you have the connections, and Kragstein has them."

"I don't know what to say about Amanda," I said, not wanting to look at Padillo, but forcing myself to.

Padillo's face tightened. "There's nothing to say."

"Yes. Well, I thought—"

"There's nothing to say," and from the way he said it, I decided that there really wasn't.

He put his drink down on the bar and again looked at me. "You didn't pick up that little gray box she was carrying, did you?"

"The one with the ring? No."

"Well, if it's worth half a million dollars, I don't suppose we should leave it lying around like that."

"No," I said. "I don't suppose we should."

It wasn't hard to find the ring. It was still in the

box and the box was still in Amanda Clarkmann's left hand. Padillo lifted the blanket away, reached down for the box, and handed it to me. He stood there, holding the blanket, and looking at Amanda Clarkmann for what seemed to be a long time. I opened the box and looked at the ring. It may have been worth a half million dollars, but just then I wouldn't have given a dime for it.

I drove out of the basement entrance and onto Sixty-fourth just as a carload of men in dark suits and white shirts got out of a black Ford Galaxie and flashed some identification at the three doormen. Two of the men looked at us and then looked away quickly, as if we were someone whom they'd cross the street to avoid meeting. Maybe we were.

Padillo sat next to me. The king and Scales were in the rear. Neither of them had said much other than some murmured condolences to Padillo about Amanda Clarkmann's death. Padillo had turned away before they were half through with their murmurings. We were just coming out of the Lincoln Tunnel when I said, "What'll we do with the car?"

"Leave it in the parking lot and mail the ticket back to William."

"I have another question."

"You worry too much."

"Only over nonessentials such as our reservations."

"What about them."

"If you made them over the phone and Kragstein was tapped in, then he knows where we're going."

"I didn't make them over the phone," Padillo said.

"Who did?"

"No one. We don't have any."

Because there is only one direct flight a day from Newark to Denver and because not too many persons seemed interested in making the trip, we had no trouble getting first-class reservations on United Flight 855 which would get us into Denver at four o'clock, just in time to make connections with United Flight 367 to Los Angeles, leaving Denver at 4:40 and arriving in Los Angeles at 5:53 providing that no one decided to go to Cuba.

Padillo turned to me and said, "How much money have you got?"

"Around five hundreds."

"Can you pay for your own ticket?"

"Sure," I said and handed over two hundred dollars. The United man gave me $13 in change. He actually owed me $13.10, but Congress now lets them round it off to the next highest dollar so if your ticket actually costs $162.02, you pay $163.00, which not only simplifies the airlines' bookkeeping, but also nets them $50 million a year. It also gives me something else to brood about.

When I looked at the ticket that Padillo had handed me I saw that my new name was R. Miller.

"What did you call our two friends?"

"F. Jones and L. Brown."

"And yours?"

"Q. Smythe—with a y and an e."

"That's real class," I said. "What's the Q stand for?"

"Quaint."

There were those who once swore by the air in Denver, claiming that it could cure anything from rickets to tuberculosis. I don't suppose they do anymore, not if that gray, greasy-looking blanket of smog that I saw out of the plane's window occurs every other day or so. I could still see the frosted mountains in the background, but the smog even made them look as though they needed to be hosed down.

"I didn't know Denver had smog," I said to Padillo. "What do they do, import it from L.A.?"

"They grow their own," he said. "Everybody does nowadays."

As soon as we were inside Stapleton Airport, the public address system started calling for Mr. Q. Smythe. "Mr. Q. Smythe, will you please report to the United Airlines information counter."

"Do you think there might be two of them?" I said.

Padillo shook his head and turned to the king and Scales. "Sit down over there," he said, motioning toward two chairs. "Don't move." He turned back to me. "You go. I don't want to leave them loose."

"Who do you think it is?"

"Somebody from Burmser."

"What do you want me to say?"

"Nothing. Just listen."

I nodded and walked to the information counter where a blond with silvered eyelids smiled at me and said that two gentlemen were waiting for me in the VIP lounge. She gave me directions to the lounge and once inside it wasn't hard to spot them. They both wore vests and no sideburns and nice, quiet ties and quiet, hard looks. I walked over to them and said, "I've got time for just one drink. A Scotch and water."

One of them had a turned-up nose and pale blue

eyes. He glanced down at a small four-by-five-inch photograph that he held in his left hand. "You don't look much like this wire-photo of Mr. Smythe, friend."

"I just take messages for him."

"We'd rather talk to Mr. Smythe," the other one said, rising from his chair. His nose leaned a little to the left, as if a football cleat might have smacked into it once. He was larger than his partner and he had brown eyes that were almost hazel. Neither of them was over thirty.

"Mr. Smythe's tied up," I said, "and I'd still like that drink."

The taller one looked at his partner and then back at me. "You McCorkle?"

I nodded. He held out his hand and I reached into my pocket and took out my billfold. Slowly. If they worked for Burmser, I didn't want to upset them. I handed him a D.C. driver's license, which had my photograph on it in color. He looked at the photograph and then at me and then back at the photograph. It wasn't all that bad. He handed the license back, turned, and signaled to a cocktail waitress who came over, smiling expectantly.

"One Scotch and water and two Cokes," he said and then motioned me to sit down across the cocktail table from them. I sat down and looked around and smiled to show how nice I thought everything was. They didn't smile back. They didn't say anything until the drinks were served and the waitress had left. I picked mine up and took a large swallow. They didn't touch theirs.

"We heard about you," the one with the snub nose said. "They said you were a semi-pro. Not quite sharp enough for the minors."

"I won't even play next year," I said. "What about the message?"

"You had trouble in New York," the tall one with the almost hazel eyes said.

"Some," I agreed.

"They can't sit on it more than forty-eight hours. Tell your Mr. Smythe that."

"All right."

"And tell him that they want both Kragstein and Gitner out of the way within forty-eight hours. Especially Gitner."

"Out of the way," I said. "Just where would that be?"

They exchanged glances and then the one with the snub nose leaned forward and said softly, "That would be dead."

"Oh."

"Have you got it?"

"It's simple enough," I said. "There's just one thing."

"What?" the taller of the two said.

"What happens after forty-eight hours if they're not out of the way?"

They rose together as if they had practiced it. Maybe they had. The one with the snub nose looked down at me and his blue eyes seemed to drop far below freezing. "What happens?" he said. "Anything that's necessary. Tell him that. Anything that's necessary."

I watched them leave while I finished my Scotch. The cocktail waitress came over and let me pay for the drinks. Back in the waiting room I found Padillo standing with his back to the wall about ten feet from the king and Scales.

"What did they want?" he said.

"They want Kragstein and Gitner dead within forty-eight hours," I said. "Especially Gitner."

Padillo looked at me and then past me, through the glass windows that faced west toward the mountains which the smog seemed to have soiled. "It's not going to take that long," he said either to himself or to the mountains. From the way he said it, I was almost glad that he wasn't talking to me.

Chapter 16

We drove all night and the king didn't get to see much of California until we got to San Jose at dawn. But he had had a good look at the Grand Canyon on our way to Los Angeles from Denver because the United Airlines pilot had circled it once and had even given a brief little lecture on its geological formation which the king seemed to find fascinating. As for the canyon itself, the king went along with everybody else and called it magnificent.

We rented a Ford Galaxie at the Los Angeles airport and Padillo drove, claiming that he knew the town better than I. But it was still nearly dark before we got to Ventura because he read a sign wrong and landed us on the Santa Monica freeway which forced us to take Alternate 101 through Malibu and Topanga Beach. Southern California to me had always been lollipop land but the route made the king happy since it let him look at the ocean.

We had a sandwich on the other side of Santa Barbara along with a flat left front tire and together they killed an hour and a half. After that Padillo and I switched off on the driving, stopping for coffee every hour or so, not going much over sixty, and talking hardly at all. After Santa Barbara the king and Scales slept most of the way.

I suppose everybody has to have a home town and San Francisco was mine although I don't think that we cared too much for each other anymore. I had been born there in the old French Hospital at Sixth and Geary and I had grown up in the Richmond District in a middle-class neighborhood which then had a large number of Russian families. I assume that it still does. We had lived on Twenty-sixth Avenue about two blocks north of Golden Gate Park. Fredl and I had once spent a week in the Bay area and I had shown her the house and the neighborhood where I had lived until I got out of George Washington High School and went into the Army, but all she had said was, "It doesn't look much like you, does it?"

I decided that over the years both the city and I have changed, perhaps neither of us for the better. San Francisco reminds me of nothing so much as a middle-aged hooker relying solely on technique now that her looks have gone. But I suspect that my real antagonism stems from being taken for a tourist in my own home town. There's nothing much worse than that.

Padillo was awake now as were the king and Scales. The Freeway isn't the most scenic approach to San Francisco, but when we neared the Ninth Street Civic Center exit, the two in the back seat got their first glimpse of the Bay Bridge on their right and later they got a look at Golden Gate Bridge, neither of which led anywhere that I wanted to go.

"I used to come up here from L.A. on weekends sometimes," Padillo said. "I knew a girl who lived on Russian Hill. She got mad when I called it Frisco."

"The natives have a lot of civic pride," I said.

"She was from New Orleans."

Padillo wanted a motel so we checked into one called the Bay View Lodge at Van Ness and Washington which, because of its in-town location, offered as expensive lodgings as we could hope to find. We got two double rooms and after Padillo made sure that the king and Scales were safely tucked away in theirs and that room service would bring them some breakfast he joined me in our room where I lay on the bed, the telephone to my ear, ordering our own breakfast which consisted of scrambled eggs, ham, rye toast, a quart or so of coffee, and two double Bloody Marys which the young lady on the other end of the telephone didn't seem to think that I really wanted at seven fifteen in the morning. I eventually won her consent, if not her approval.

Padillo took the automatic from his waistband and slipped it under the pillow before lying down on the other bed. He folded his arms beneath his head and stared at the ceiling. I lit a cigarette, which tasted foul, and blew some smoke at the spot on the ceiling that Padillo stared at.

"Now what?" I said.

"First we get some sleep."

"Have we got time for that?"

"We'll take it."

"And then."

"Then I locate Wanda and find out where she wants those two delivered and when."

"Do you know where she is?"

"What's the most fashionable hotel in town, the Fairmont?"

I thought a moment. "I think it's a toss-up between that and the St. Francis."

"Then I won't have any trouble finding Wanda."

"Neither will Kragstein and Gitner."

"I'm counting on it," Padillo said.

* * *

It was Rhododendron Week in Union Square across from the St. Francis and the bronze figure of Victory, perched on its ten-story granite shaft, rose out of a calm sea of showy blooms that were purple and pink and white. I remembered that the city always tried to keep Union Square full of flowers, but during Rhododendron Week in April they carted in tubs of them until the whole thing looked as if it were drenched with blossoms. The figure of Victory commemorates a win for our side in Southeast Asia, but it's for when Dewey smashed the Spanish Fleet in Manila Bay which means that it's nothing to toss your hat up in the air about now.

They built the St. Francis in 1907 right after the earthquake and over the years it has carefully preserved its neo-Renaissance elegance. With the prices that it charges it can afford to. Wanda Gothar had a two-room suite on the seventh floor, but except for some flowers that the hotel must have supplied, the suite looked just as impersonal and unoccupied as did her room at the Hay-Adams in Washington. I decided that she probably made a hit with hotel maids.

"You'll want a drink, of course," she said.

"If it's no bother," I said, moving to the window to see whether the suite had something of a view. It faced on the square and she could look down at the lake of rhododendrons to her heart's content. The flowers appeared even gaudier from seven floors up, but it was a cheerful kind of flashiness that nobody could really object to.

"Padillo mentioned that you had trouble in New York," she said as she came back into the living room, carrying two drinks. She handed me one of them. "He said you could tell me about it."

I tasted my drink. It was Scotch and water. "They tried twice," I said. "The second time they almost made it. Gitner killed the woman whose apartment we were using. She was a good friend of Padillo's."

"Is he upset? Oh, I don't mean upset. He wouldn't show it if he were. He wouldn't know how. I meant to ask is it something personal with him now?"

"He's upset and it's personal," I said.

She nodded and lowered herself to the edge of a divan that was upholstered in green and white stripes. She moved as she always did, with grace and poise, but with a hesitancy that I hadn't noticed before, as if she were listening for inaudible stage directions. Perhaps from her brother.

"He'll go after Gitner, of course."

"It seems that way."

"And he'll try to use the king as bait."

"He'll use whatever's on hand," I said.

"Yes. The king. Or you. Or me."

"She was rather special to him."

"The woman in New York?"

"Yes."

She nodded before taking a sip of her drink. "I know what that can mean."

I could have taken her remark several ways, but I decided not to take it at all. "Padillo wants to know where and when you want them delivered."

She put her drink down, picked up a cigarette and lit it before I could move more than a foot or two from my spot by the window. I decided to sit down and chose a comfortable-looking lounge chair. Wanda Gothar smoked her cigarette for several moments before saying anything.

"Padillo's keeping watch, I assume."

"Yes."

"They wouldn't like anything to go wrong."

"They?"

"The oil companies."

"Which ones?"

She told me and I felt like whistling my surprise. Instead I took another swallow of my drink. When most persons think of oil towns, they think of Dallas and Houston and Tulsa and perhaps Los Angeles. For some reason San Francisco isn't regarded as one. But down where Mechanics Square used to be were two buildings, one twenty-two stories tall, the other twenty-nine, which housed two of the world's largest oil companies, one of them founded by a skinny old man who had lived for almost a century and whose heirs are among the richest people in the world. The other oil company, almost as big, was established by a European banking family whose spare cash more than once has been used to shore up tottering governments. At last count, the company that was founded by the skinny old man had overseas operations in seventy countries. Its other claim to immortality was that it had launched the world's first filling station in Seattle back in 1907. The company that the European banking family controlled operated in nearly as many foreign countries and I decided that if there was enough oil underneath the sands of Llaquah to make a joint venture attractive to both firms, then the king had seriously underpriced himself with his demand for five million dollars in earnest money.

Five million to them was probably a half hour's income on a slow day.

"Which firm plays host?" I said.

"The one on the north side of Bush Street," she said. "It was what the meeting in Dallas was largely about. They both wanted the honor."

"What did they say when you told them that there was a large chance that the king wouldn't make it to the ceremonies?"

"They smiled," she said. "They smiled and then they got a distant look in their eyes. It's surprising how much alike those oil men look."

"What kind of smiles?" I said.

"Polite smiles. Indifferent smiles. They may have been thinking about what kind of agreement they could make with Kassim's successor. That oil isn't going anywhere."

"Maybe they didn't believe you," I said.

She shrugged. "Perhaps."

"When do they want the king there?"

"Tomorrow morning at ten. The twenty-ninth floor."

"All right," I said and rose. "Anything else?"

"Tell Padillo that I'll join you at six this evening."

"For an all-night vigil?"

"Something like that."

"He's expecting company."

"I know. Gitner and Kragstein."

"That doesn't bother you?"

"On the contrary, I look forward to it."

"Why? Because you think they killed your brother?"

"Don't you? Doesn't Padillo?"

"He hasn't said."

"But you, Mr. McCorkle, what do you think?"

"Just one thing," I said. "But it's not conjecture, it's fact, and I don't much like it because it still bothers me."

"What bothers you?"

"That whoever killed your brother killed him in my living room."

A pale blue Pontiac sedan followed my taxi from the St. Francis to the Bay View Lodge Motel. There were two men in the Pontiac, but I didn't recognize them, and they didn't try to disguise the fact that they were following me, which was just as well because that was the way that Padillo had planned it earlier that afternoon.

Chapter 17

Padillo was still lying on the bed and still examining the ceiling when I entered the motel room.

"You called it," I said. "They picked me up just as I left the St. Francis."

"Gitner and Kragstein?" he asked, as if he expected me to say no.

"Two I didn't recognize. They were driving a Pontiac. A light blue one, if it makes any difference."

"What did Wanda say?"

I told him all about the meeting that was scheduled for ten the next morning and as he listened he kept his eyes on the ceiling, not moving, rarely blinking, not even smoking. When I finally stopped talking, he sat up slowly, his hands still clasped behind his head, and then, with his legs fully extended, touched each elbow to his knees.

"What's that, your exercise for the year?"

"I just wanted to see whether I could still do it."

"Doesn't it hurt?"

"No," he said and looked a little surprised. "Is it supposed to?"

"Only those who deserve it—like me."

"She say anything else?"

"Wanda?"

He nodded, swung his feet off the bed, and rose.

"Just that she's joining us at six and that she's

convinced that Kragstein and Gitner killed her brother."

"That's a theory anyway," Padillo said as he reached under the pillow for his automatic. "She needs one."

"You've got your own, of course."

"I'm still working on it," he said.

We went next door where the king and Scales were watching a fifteen-year-old movie that seemed to be about the good times that could be had down on a subsistence farm. Scales switched it off when we came in and looked a little embarrassed. The king looked only disappointed.

He also looked less like a king than ever. He was sprawled on one of the twin beds, wearing only slacks and a T-shirt. The T-shirt seemed fairly clean but it had a hole in its side. The king's belly strained at the shirt and he was comforting himself with a giant-size Baby Ruth. Other than that he needed a shave he appeared to be as placid and content as ever and I had the feeling that he had all the makings of a first-class benevolent despot.

Padillo had never cared much for preambles, so he began at the crux of things. "They're going to try to kill you between now and ten o'clock tomorrow morning," he said. The king choked on a mouthful of Baby Ruth, but recovered nicely. Scales, seated in a chair near the TV set, crossed his legs the other way to show that he was concerned.

Now that he had their attention Padillo told them what Wanda Gothar had told me. When he was through he looked at the king and said, "I'm going to say it just one more time. If I were you, I'd ask for police protection. If you have some aversion to the local police, then I suggest that you request protection from the Secret Service or the FBI or even some other Federal agency. All it takes is a phone call. If you were really smart, you'd not only ask for that, but also for a cell in the city jail tonight."

The king bit off another bite from his candy bar, chewed it thoroughly, swallowed, and then said in a soft, reproachful voice, "The jail in Dallas did not afford much protection for the Oswald person, Mr. Padillo. Forgive me, but I have little faith in your jails or your police or your Mr. Herbert Hoover."

"J. Edgar," Padillo said. "Herbert's dead.'"

"Yes. J. Edgar."

"So you won't change your mind?"

The king shook his head. Stubbornly, I thought. "No, I will not change my mind. I have every confidence in you and Miss Gothar." He paused and then added quickly, "And Mr. McCorkle, of course." I decided that when Kassim became king, the diplomatic corps had suffered no great loss.

"You agree with this, Scales?" Padillo said.

"I think his Majesty's point is well taken. Furthermore, Mr. Padillo, I feel that you and your colleagues have just been paid a great compliment—one that you will remember in years to come."

"Especially if he gets killed tonight," Padillo said. He looked at his watch. "It's five o'clock now. That means we have seventeen hours to go before the ceremony takes place. I don't know when Kragstein and Gitner will try it. Maybe as soon as it gets dark. Or at three o'clock in the morning or even on the way down to the oil company. They may even try it more than once, but that seems unlikely if they want to avoid the cops. So I want neither of you to move out of this room between now and tomorrow morning. Your food will be brought to you by either McCorkle or me. You're to answer the door to no one but us. You are not to answer the phone or to make any calls. If something happens, try to get to the bathroom and lock yourself in. That might give you a minute or two and that minute or two could make the difference between whether you're dead or alive. If you have any questions, you'd better ask them now."

It had been a long speech for Padillo and both the king and Scales seemed to have followed it closely. When he was done, they looked at each other, and the king shook his head slightly.

"We have no questions," Scales said. "His Majesty's safety is in your hands."

Padillo looked as though he wanted to say something, something rude, even nasty, but apparently thought better of it. He turned and moved to the door where he turned once again and looked back at the king. "I think—" he said and then stopped. Instead he pointed at the door. "Be sure to lock and bolt this after we're gone."

When we were back in our own room I said, "What were you going to tell him before you changed your mind?"

"That he was a damned fool. But you don't tell kings that, do you?"

"Not unless they are—but if they are, it doesn't do any good."

Wanda Gothar arrived promptly at six, carrying a large dark brown leather purse and wearing shoes that matched, a dun-colored pantsuit that would have looked drab on anyone else, and a concerned expression.

"I think I was followed," she said, "but I couldn't be sure because of the traffic."

"It doesn't matter," Padillo said. "They know we're here."

He was back on his bed, inspecting the ceiling again. He hadn't risen when Wanda came in. I indicated that she should have the chair that I'd been sitting in and she lowered herself into it as she glanced around the room with a look that gave it a C-minus rating.

After inspecting the room she turned her gaze on Padillo who fared no better. She placed a cigarette in her mouth, but I didn't bother to try to light it this time.

"Well," she said after blowing some smoke out in a long, gray plume, "when do you think they'll try it?"

"Before ten o'clock tomorrow," Padillo said to the ceiling.

"That's no answer."

"It's the best I have."

"You know how Kragstein works," she said. "What's his preference?"

"He doesn't have any. That's what's kept him alive. Morning, noon, or night. They're all the same to him. You were two years old when he started in this business, Wanda, so don't try to outguess him."

"Walter didn't think that he was quite as good as you paint him."

"And Walter's dead, isn't he?" Padillo said.

I thought that Padillo shouldn't have said it. It seemed to be one of those needlessly cruel remarks that you would like to recall and disown as soon as they're uttered. Wanda Gothar flinched slightly, but when she spoke her voice was low and controlled. "Is that why your friend in New York is dead, Padillo? Because you underestimated Kragstein?"

Padillo sat up on the edge of the bed and stared at the floor for a moment before turning his head to look at Wanda. "I deserved that, I suppose."

I felt that it was as close as he would come to an apology, but it didn't mollify Wanda. "But you did underestimate him?"

"Not really," he said. "I was faked out by too much money. It takes the edge off and gives you a false sense of security. That's what it's for, of course. So I let it lull me and Kragstein was smart enough to figure it out." He stopped looking at Wanda, reached for a cigarette and lit it, and when he spoke again, he seemed to be talking more to himself than to us. "To stay in this business you have to stay poor. I don't know any rich ones, not any who lived long enough to spend their money if they stayed in it. Kragstein's been at it for thirty years and he still has to scramble around for next month's rent. But he's still alive."

"So are you," Wanda said.

"But someone is dead back in New York because eighty million dollars made me careless, although not careless enough to get myself killed. You're right there. But careless enough so that I had to make a choice instinctively and I don't like to make them that way. I chose to live and let Gitner's bullets kill someone else."

"It wasn't a choice," I said. "It was an automatic reaction, a reflex."

Padillo turned to look over his shoulder at me. "Was it?"

"I saw it," I said. "I saw the whole thing."

"You saw me depend on a high-priced security system that had grown flabby because nobody like Gitner had ever taken it on. It was a system designed to discourage the gentleman jewel thief who'd be afraid to go up against it because he might get his dinner jacket mussed. I made my mistake when I believed that it would keep somebody like Gitner from getting where he wanted to go. He probably thought it was quaint. I know that's what he thinks I am."

"Aren't you?" Wanda Gothar said. "Oh, not just you, Padillo, but all of us. Aren't we something like the characters in a post-World War II set piece? A trifle grim as we brood about revenge, but a little self-conscious about being here at all, and rather ashamed, I'd say, for having so quickly become such anachronisms. You're right. Quaint *is* the word."

Padillo rose and walked over to Wanda Gothar and looked down at her for several moments and then smiled. It wasn't his usual quick, hard grin. It was an almost gentle smile, one that he seemed to have been saving for a sentimental occasion on the off chance that he might have to attend one some day.

"You're not old enough to be quaint, Wanda, but you're still young enough to get out."

It was the second and last time I ever saw her smile and she still didn't put much into it, perhaps because she didn't want to waste what little was left. But still, it was a smile, and some of it seemed to creep into her voice. "You're forgetting something, Padillo."

"What?"

"The Gothar tradition, the one that goes back almost a hundred and seventy years. You know what it means?"

"Not really."

"It means that I've always been too old to get out."

The motel was a U-shaped affair, two stories high, built of redwood and glass and some kind of stone that looked too pretty to be real although it was. Our room and the one that Scales and the king occupied were at the bottom of the U. Padillo had rented two more rooms. One of them was on the right-hand side of the U on the second floor. The other one was on the ground floor on the U's left-hand side.

Padillo handed Wanda Gothar a room key and she dropped it into her purse. It clunked against something metallic.

"What are you carrying?" he said.

"A Smith and Wesson thirty-eight."

"That's all?"

"No. A Walther PPK. It was my brother's."

"Which one?"

"Paul."

"I seem to remember that he did like a Walther." He turned to me. "You know what the PPK stands for?"

"*Polizei* something," I said.

"*Polizei Pistole Kriminal.* They're both a lot of gun for you, Wanda."

"I know how to use them," she said. "Or don't you remember?"

"I remember. You get the upstairs room."

She nodded. "McCorkle will be downstairs on the

left. I'll be upstairs on the right and so you have a crossfire. Where will you be, in with them?"

"If I were in with them when it happens, it would be too late for me to do any good. I'll be here. You want to see them before you go up?"

She rose, shaking her head. "Is it necessary?"

"No."

"Then I see no point in it unless they need reassurance. Do they?"

"No."

She turned and started for the door, but stopped, and looked back at Padillo.

"Tell me something."

"What?"

"You're not putting me up there because it's the farthest and presumably the safest place, are you?"

"No."

"But you do have a reason?"

"Yes. I have a reason."

"Well?"

"You shoot better than McCorkle."

"Yes," she said. "That's what I thought it was."

Chapter 18

It was nearly dark and the April fog was settling down for the evening as I walked Wanda Gothar to the stairs that led to the second floor.

"You should have brought a coat," I said.

"I'm not cold." She stopped at the stairs and looked up at me. Curiously, I thought. "Why are you here, McCorkle? This isn't your métier."

"My wife's out of town," I said. It was as good an answer as any.

"Is she pretty?" Before I could reply, Wanda Gothar nodded thoughtfully and said, "Yes, she would be. You'd need that." She looked at my face some more, studying it as if she hoped to discover some vanished trace of character. "Children?" she said.

"No."

"Are you planning on any?"

"The demand for them seems to have slacked off."

"And you're faithful to your wife." It wasn't a question.

"Being unfaithful is hard work and I work hard to avoid that."

"Was Padillo in love with her?"

"Who?" I knew whom she meant, but I was trying to think up an answer.

"The woman in New York."

"He seemed to like her a lot."

"And she was rich."

"Very."

"That could have stopped him."

"From what?"

"From marrying her. Did you ever notice that in some ways he's frightfully old-fashioned?"

"No."

"If he weren't concerned about such an outdated emotion as revenge, we wouldn't be here." She made a small gesture that took in the motel. "This is no sanctuary, it's a trap. There must be a great many places to hide in San Francisco. He could easily have found one."

"Why don't you tell him?"

"Because," she said, "I'm even more old-fashioned than he is."

She turned and started up the stairs to her room. From the rear she looked as old-fashioned as next week. But perhaps she was right, I thought, as I made my way around the heated, Olympic-sized swimming pool that no one was swimming in, and headed for the room that Padillo had rented for me, the one from which I could pot away at Kragstein and Gitner with the office .38 if they ever showed up. And if I could see them in the fog. And if I didn't fall asleep.

Revenge might be an old-fashioned emotion or motive or whatever it was, I thought, as I tossed the room key onto the plastic topped writing desk, but it still drew all sorts of people into all sorts of trouble. It could make a wispy little housewife chuckle as she splashed acid in the Other Woman's face. A fifty-year-old accountant grinned at midnight while he stuffed the money into the suitcase and thought about the look on the boss's face when it was discovered that the monthly payroll was on its way to Rio. And I had seen the self-righteousness in the face of the steady customer who had sped out to Chevy Chase to pick up his shotgun so that he could come back and blow the head off the waiter who had spilled the veal Niçoise all over the wife's new dress.

That type of revenge was based on rage which, if heated to just the right temperature, can make any action, no matter how foolish, seem coldly logical and completely justified—even slamming the six-week-old baby against the wall because it won't stop crying.

But there was nothing impetuous in the way that Wanda Gothar and Padillo sought their revenge. They went about it dispassionately, purposely setting a weak-jawed trap and then installing themselves as part of the bait. I decided that I didn't want either one of them miffed at me.

I turned a chair around at the window, mixed a drink from a pint of Scotch that I'd bought in Los Angeles, turned off the lights, and settled down to watch the entrance of the motel. I even took the revolver out of my jacket pocket and laid it on a convenient table next to my chair so that I could reach it easily when I needed to shoot someone.

After an hour of this I went over to the phone and asked the desk to ring Padillo's room. When he answered, I said, "You forgot something."

"What?"

"The magic glasses. I can't see through the fog."

"I've noticed," he said. "You're the native, do you think it'll lift?"

"Not tonight."

"It could be to our advantage."

"How?"

"Kragstein may not want to try it in the fog."

"You're the expert," I said.

"I'm just trying to think like Kragstein."

"Is it hard?"

"Not if you have a nasty turn of mind."

"What you're saying is that he could keep us up all night and then try it in the morning when he's fresh and we're pinching ourselves to keep awake."

"That's what he could hope that we think."

"And if we do," I said, "it could make us careless."

"Especially around three or four o'clock in the morning."

"So either way we stay awake," I said.

"That's right."

"All night."

"All night. What's your visibility now?"

"Wait a second," I said and crossed over to the window and peered out. Across the swimming pool I could still see the glow of the light above the room that the king and Scales occupied. Their curtains were drawn and I could see no shadows moving behind them. Perhaps they had already locked themselves in the bathroom.

I went back to the phone and said, "If the inspector's hansom cab draws up, I'll be able to tell what it is, but that's about all. I'd say that I've got about forty percent visibility, but it's going to get worse."

"How much worse?"

"I'm not the weather bureau."

"Guess."

"All right, I'll guess that it'll get so bad within an hour that I won't even be able to see the swimming pool."

"Christ," Padillo said. He was silent for a moment

while he sorted out the alternatives. Or options, since he lived in Washington. "We're going to have to feed them."

"Don't forget the hired help."

"Okay. I'll call room service and order some hamburgers and coffee. They can deliver Wanda's and mine. You can deliver to the king and Scales. If the fog's worse after we eat, you and I will move in with them and Wanda can take my room."

"There's just one other thing," I said.

"What?"

"I want onions on mine."

The room service waiter who brought the hamburgers and coffee was a sad-eyed youth whose despondency seemed to stem from society's failure to recognize his true potential.

"You know what they call this?" he said. "They call this on-the-job training. I'm supposed to be learning it from the ground up."

"The motel business?" I said, watching him slam the tray down on top of the television set.

"Motel management, they call it. Down at the employment service they claim it's got a real future. I already been here three weeks and ain't learned a damn thing."

"That's too bad," I said. "How much?"

"Six hamburgers and three coffees. That's twelve-eighty-six with tax."

It was an exorbitant tab, but there was no sense in arguing with the help so I handed him three fives and then watched him fumble around in his pocket for change. He gave me a small embarrassed laugh and even managed to blush a little. "I ain't got any change," he said, looking so wretched and apologetic that I almost wanted to pat him on the shoulder.

"I didn't think that you would."

"I can run get it."

"Don't bother," I said. "You know, if you get tired of this job, they've got some fairly good acting schools down in L.A."

He made himself look both interested and grateful. "You think they might let me in?"

"No, but they might let you teach."

After he had gone I put my own food aside to cool and carried the tray containing the rest over to the king and Scales. I knocked on the door three times, announcing loudly that it was McCorkle. I could hear the bolt and lock being undone and after Scales made me tell him three more times who it was he opened the door.

"Hamburgers and coffee," I said, entering the room and putting the tray down on the writing desk. The king was sitting in a chair, fully dressed. Scales was hovering around, still wearing his worn blue suit. He looked even more seedy than usual.

"The fog, Mr. McCorkle," Scales said, "will it get worse?"

"Probably. If it does, Padillo and I are going to move in with you after we eat."

The king was already devouring one of the hamburgers and he didn't mind talking with his mouth full. He wanted to know whether the fog would be an advantage to us or to them. At least that's what I thought he asked.

"To them," I said. "We have to stay awake no matter what. They don't. They can take a nice nap and then use the fog as cover."

"When do you think that they'll—"

"I have no idea," I said. "Just keep your door locked until we get here."

Walking back to my room I noticed that the fog had grown thicker even in the short time that I had been with Scales and the king. When I was inside I put the revolver back on the table, placed the hamburgers and coffee next to it, and sat down to watch, wait and eat. There wasn't much to watch now because I could no longer see the light that burned above the room where the two men waited for someone to kill them. Or try to. One car drove in and went past on its way to a room two doors down from mine, but I could see only its headlights.

I was finishing the last of the coffee when there was a knock on my door. It was Padillo. He came in wearing a sour look and shaking his head.

"It's worse," he said.

"I know."

"I'm going to get Wanda. You may as well rejoin them."

"All right."

I put the revolver back in my pocket and we started around the swimming pool. Another car entered the motel drive and moved slowly past my room, then headed toward the end of the U-shaped drive. I couldn't tell what kind of car it was or how many people it contained. Both of us watched it carefully. When the car rounded the end of the U, it cut its lights, but we could tell from the sound of its engine that it was still moving, heading up the other arm of the U-shaped drive, heading toward the room occupied by Scales and the king.

We were still at the pool, halfway from either of its ends, when the driver gunned the car's engine once as if to pick up speed. We could see nothing until he applied the brakes and the band of red lights across the car's rear sent a ruby glow through the fog.

Padillo was already racing around the pool. He swore as he ran. We rounded the pool's far end just as the explosion ripped through the fog. It was a deep, harsh cracking blast, far too loud for a shot. Before its echo died away there was another blast and then a third and after the echoes there was nothing but silence until two car doors slammed. The dull red glow of the car taillights blinked off and the engine screamed and whined as the driver jammed the accelerator to the floor and shot the car toward the motel entrance.

By then we were at the room that Scales and the king occupied. Padillo had his gun out, but there was no longer anything to shoot at. He looked disappointed. Some people had popped out of doors and were asking the fog and each other and the night what had happened, but none of them seemed to know. The door to the room had been blown off its hinges and into the driveway. We entered the room quickly and saw that the bathroom door also had been ripped from its fastenings, but the bathroom light had somehow escaped. It was the only light there was.

The bed nearest the outside door had received a direct hit and the foam rubber of its mattress littered the room. The writing desk was smashed as were the chairs. There were no longer any pictures on the walls. The innards of the smashed TV set were smoking. Padillo went into the bathroom and came back with a glass of water. He poured it on the TV set and it hissed for a few moments.

There was nothing salvageable left. The mirror

that had hung above the writing desk now lay in tiny pieces on the floor. There was no glass in the windows. There was something brown splashed on the walls just above the ruined writing desk, but on close inspection it turned out to be coffee.

Padillo turned slowly, giving the mess that was the room a careful survey as he stuck the automatic back into the waistband of his trousers. My revolver was still in my jacket pocket because I had forgotten about it again. Padillo turned to look at me, shaking his head in mild disbelief and disgust that seemed not so mild. The disbelief was directed at the room, the disgust at himself.

"What's wrong with this picture?" he said.

"It lacks a little something. Such as gore."

"No blood-spattered walls. No unattached limbs lying about."

"Which means," I said, "that there was nobody home."

"It also means something else."

"What?"

"We've been sacked. Fired."

I gave the room another elaborate glance. "We probably deserved it. That's just an offhand opinion, of course."

Padillo bent down and picked up a piece of blackened foam rubber and sniffed it before tossing it away. "Grenades. Three of them."

"I thought I heard three."

Padillo looked about the room once more, as if searching for something, perhaps a farewell note. "They had to have some reason."

"The king and Scales?"

He nodded.

"Reason for what?"

"For running out on us."

I gave the room one last final look. What hadn't been demolished had been ruined. "If they had a reason," I said, "I think I know what kind it was."

"What kind?"

"A sound one."

Chapter 19

Padillo and Wanda Gothar waited in the Ford while I went into the motel office where the sad-eyed young room service waiter was holding down the front desk. The night manager was back at the bombed-out room, clucking his tongue over the damage and waiting for the police to arrive.

"Hey, didja hear those bombs?" the young man asked. "Big boom, huh?"

"I was over there," I said.

"Didja know those two guys?"

"Just casually. They said they had to catch a plane and gave me some money to take care of any charges they might have run up."

"They didn't have no charges," he said. "That was the first thing Hinckle checked. Hinckle's the night manager."

"He didn't check with me," a woman's voice said. I turned and a middle-aged woman with frosted hair and green eyeshadow glared at me from her post at the switchboard. "I got T and C on that long-distance call they made and didn't pay for."

"T and C's time and charges," the young man said, assuming my ignorance.

I reached for my wallet. "I'll be glad to pay it."

"They should've paid it themselves," the woman said. "A lot of people think they can skip out on their phone bills here just because it's a motel and they have to pay in advance. The telephone company don't like it either."

"To hell with the phone company," the young man said, but not too loudly.

"If you'll just give me the time and charges," I said.

"We're gonna start making people put their home phone numbers down when they register," the woman said. "Then if they call Honolulu or New York and try to skip out without paying, they'll get stuck for it when they get their monthly bill. The phone company said they'd cooperate."

"That's Mrs. Hinckle," the young man said. "She used to work for the phone company. She thinks it's the greatest thing in the world. You know what I think?"

"What?"

"I think it's a monopoly and I got a way to beat it."

"How?" I said, interested in spite of myself.

"You know how when you get your monthly bill the phone company sends along an envelope that you can mail your payment back to them in?"

I nodded.

"Well, all those envelopes got on it is just their name. Not yours, just theirs. So you know what I do?"

"No."

He looked around as if he were about to slip me the formula for transforming lead into gold. "I don't put no stamp on it," he whispered. "And they gotta pay for it." He went on hurriedly, still whispering. "Now suppose everybody did this. How many people got phones, maybe fifty, a hundred million?"

"Say fifty."

"So fifty million times six cents is how much? That's three million dollars a month the phone company gotta pay in postage due if everybody did it."

"Ingenious," I said. "I'll spread the word."

"We gotta start small, but it's coming."

"What?"

"The revolution, man."

Mrs. Hinckle bore down on me, clutching a slip of paper. "Number twenty-six owes eleven dollars and twenty-eight cents for a call to Washington. That's D.C., not the state."

I handed her fifteen dollars. "Could I have a receipt, please?"

She nodded and went back to her switchboard. From outside, I could hear the wail of a police siren. I estimated it to be two blocks away. "And the number that was called, too, if you don't mind."

She looked up and glared at me again, but nodded, and kept on writing. I thanked her when she handed me the receipt and she managed a "You're welcome." As I turned away, the would-be revolutionary whispered. "Don't forget about the phone bill deal."

"I couldn't," I said. "It's a great step forward."

On the way to the Ford I looked at the Washington number that Mrs. Hinckle had written on the receipt. I didn't recognize it, but I have a bad memory for phone numbers. Just as I opened the door on the driver's side, the police car swept into the motel entrance, its siren dying with a reluctant moan. The two uniformed cops gave me a quick glance, but apparently saw nothing that interested them. I got in the car quickly, started the engine, and headed down Van Ness. Wanda Gothar was in front, Padillo in back. I handed him the receipt.

"They made a call to Washington," I said. "Does that number mean anything to you?"

He read it, said no, and handed it up to Wanda. She shook her head and gave it back to me. "They must have talked for five or six minutes at least," I said.

"All right," Padillo said, "let's go to the St. Francis."

"You don't think that you're going to find them there, do you?" Wanda said, not trying to conceal the sarcasm in her voice.

"I'm not trying to find them right now," he said. "At ten o'clock tomorrow that'll be easy. The king'll be down at the oil company with his fountain pen uncapped—if he's still alive. But sometime between now and then Kragstein is going to learn that those three grenades didn't kill anybody. So he's going to start looking. First, he'll look for the king and Scales and when he can't find them, he's going to start looking for us. I want to make it easy for him and the St. Francis will be the first place he'll look because he knows that's where you've been staying."

Wanda Gothar turned around in the seat so that she could face Padillo. "For the last ten minutes I've been asking you questions and you haven't had any answers. You don't know why Kassim and Scales vanished. You don't know where they might have gone. You don't even know how they managed to slip by you."

"Fog," I said. "A pair of elephants could have slipped by."

"They weren't elephants," she snapped. "They were two men who're none too smart and not nearly clever. Something frightened them or forced them into flight and it's good that it did because otherwise they'd be dead. What's the matter with you, Padillo? Are you so preoccupied with revenging that dead woman in New York that you can't keep your mind on the job at hand?"

"I made a mistake, Wanda. Let's leave it at that." I couldn't see his face, but I was sure that I knew what it looked like—stiff and drawn with his mouth stretched into that thin, hard line.

"We'd better find them," she said.

"It's a big town," I said. "By now they could be in Berkeley or Sausalito or even Oakland, although God knows why anyone would go there. I don't mind spending the night looking, but if I do, I want to know that I'm at least warm if not red-hot."

"We've only got one lead so let's try it," Padillo said.

"The Washington phone number?" Wanda asked.

"If we have any other lead, nobody's told me about it."

After I let Wanda and Padillo out in front of the St. Francis, I put the car in the underground lot beneath Union Square and joined them in Wanda's suite. Padillo tossed me a key. "You've got a new room," he said.

"What about the name?"

"It's your old one. We're no longer hiding."

"Did you call the Washington number?"

"Not yet." He turned to Wanda. "You want to call or do you want me to?"

"You call," she said. "It's your lead."

The phone permitted direct dialing so Padillo got outside and then dialed the ten numbers. We all listened while the phone rang. The room was quiet and I could hear the voice that answered in Washington, but I couldn't hear what it said. But it said the same thing twice and then Padillo slowly hung up the phone.

"It was the Llaquah Embassy," he said.

There was a silence that grew until I diplomatically broke it with, "I think I'll have a drink on that."

Wanda Gothar nodded and went into the bedroom, reappearing with three drinks on a small tray. Padillo accepted his and moved over to the window which offered a good view of the fog. I sat on the green and white striped sofa. Wanda was in a club chair with her hand that held the drink resting on its arm. Her head was back and her eyes were closed. No one seemed to have anything to say.

After several minutes of silence Padillo turned from the window, his face expressionless.

"As a lead, how good is it?" Wanda asked, not opening her eyes.

"It might narrow the search," he said.

She opened her eyes. "How?"

Padillo turned to me. "Has San Francisco got an Arab quarter or section or neighborhood?"

"I don't remember, if I ever knew, but I can find out." I moved over to the phone and asked for information. "There's a guy I used to know with UPI."

"If that intuitive leap of yours is correct, Padillo," she said, "it may tell us where they've gone, but not why."

He turned back to the window. "There's a possibility that I know that, too," he said.

"But you're going to keep it to yourself."

"Yes."
"Why?"
"Because it's still just a possibility."

There were a lot of representatives of what has been called the Arab world in San Francisco. There were Algerians and Egyptians and a large number of Syrians and Jordanians. There were a few Tunisians, I learned, and some Saudi Arabians.

"What about Armenians?" the man from UPI asked. "We've got a lot of Armenians."

"I'd say that they're geographically unacceptable."

"Saroyan's an Armenian," he said, trying to be helpful.

"I thought there might be a section or a neighborhood where they congregated."

"Not really," he said. "They're all sort of scattered around."

"Do you know of any from Llaquah?"

"Where the hell's Llaquah?"

"Not too far from Kuwait."

"What do you call somebody from Llaquah?"

"A Llaquahian," I said. "It rhymes with Hawaiian."

"Well, I don't know of any Llaquahians, but that doesn't mean there aren't some. If you really want to find out, there's a restaurant that a lot of the Middle East types hang out in."

"What's it called?"

"The Arabian Knight. That's knight with a k."

"I was afraid of that."

We hung up after promising each other that we'd get together for a drink before I went back to Washington. Both of us knew that we wouldn't.

* * *

The Arabian Knight restaurant was near Eighteenth and Querrero Streets in the Mission District and I remembered it as an area of German bakeries, Greek and Italian restaurants, a couple of Russian bars, and a sizable number of people who claimed to be from Malta. Now there was a rash of *Se Habla Español* signs in the shop windows so I assumed that a lot of persons of Spanish descent had moved back into the area which was named for the Misión San Francisco de Asís, founded five days before a group of malcontents in Philadelphia got around to issuing their Declaration of Independence.

Despite its name, San Francisco has about as much Spanish flavor as a bagel. Although widely admired for its high suicide rate, its nicely rising incidence of alcoholism, its occasional riot, and its cosmopolitan atmosphere, the city hasn't done much about promoting its Spanish heritage. No doubt it will as soon as somebody figures out how it can bring a fast dollar.

We parked the car and walked back to the Arabian Knight which occupied the lower half of a two-story building whose front someone had gussied up with Permastone. Inside it was smoky and dark and crowded. There was a long bar, a row of high-backed booths, and some tables covered with red and white checkered oilcloth which helped cut down on the laundry bill.

The door to the kitchen was open and either customers or waiters wandered in and out. I couldn't tell the difference. A jukebox blared out some Mideast music, marching songs for all I knew. There were only a few women in the place. The male customers sat in the booths or at tables in groups of three and four, drinking coffee and arrack and beer, their faces only a few inches apart, shouting at each other over the noise of the jukebox, probably conspiring against Israel.

A swarthy, slim man of about thirty who wore a white shirt and a narrow black tie came up to us and yelled to determine whether we wanted a booth or a table. Padillo yelled booth and we were led back to one which was close enough to the kitchen for us to hear the cooks arguing with the waiters.

The waiter handed Padillo a menu and Padillo handed it back, saying that we only wanted drinks—arrack for the three of us. The waiter nodded, left, and when he returned, Padillo asked if the owner was around. The waiter nodded again, pointed to the last booth, bent down, and yelled "Dr. Asfourh!" Padillo brought out a card, the one which said only, "Michael Padillo, Washington, D.C.," and handed it to the waiter, and asked him to find out whether Dr. Asfourh could spare us a few moments. In private. The waiter looked dubious, but went away, came back, and screamed that Dr. Asfourh would see us in his office upstairs in ten minutes. It came out in a short series of screams really. "Dr. Asfourh—upstairs—he see you—ten minutes." He held up all of his fingers to make sure that we got it straight.

Wanda Gothar sat next to me in the booth. She leaned toward Padillo and raised her voice so that both of us could hear. "I'll stay here."

Padillo looked at her, a little strangely, I thought. "Why?" he said.

"You were about to leave your flanks unprotected again. It's getting to be a habit with you, isn't it?"

"I don't think so."

"Think again. How many tries have Kragstein and Gitner made, five?"

"Four," Padillo said. "One in Delaware, two in New York, and one here."

"And how many people are dead?"

"Two. One of theirs and a friend of mine."

"Two of theirs might be in the hospital," I said. "My contribution."

"My brother," she said. "You forgot Walter."

Padillo shook his head. "I didn't forget Walter, I just didn't mention him."

"Why?"

"Because," Padillo said, "I don't think Kragstein and Gitner killed him."

Chapter 20

If Wanda Gothar wanted to ask Padillo if he thought he knew who had killed her brother, she didn't get the chance because he rose, turned, and headed for the door just behind the last booth. The door opened onto a flight of stairs. I followed my leader.

At the top of the stairs there was a grimy hall that needed to be swept. Padillo hesitated before turning right or left and then turned right when a rich bass voice called out, "This way, Mr. Padillo."

That way was down the hall toward the rear of the building. Pale amber light flooded through a half-open door. We went through it and into a room that seemed to have been decorated by someone enthralled with Egyptian antiquity. There was a large, authentic-looking statue of Osiris, king of the dead, which was flanked by one of his sister-wife Isis—the goddess of fertility, I remembered from somewhere. An old movie, probably. The rugs were also from the Middle East, Lebanon no doubt, and looked expensive.

The room had no windows that I could see, but that may have been because heavy amber drapes that looked like real silk covered two of its walls. The indirect lighting revealed some other Egyptian artifacts which I felt should have been in a museum: there was a large fresco that hung on one wall and looked as if it might have been stolen from the ceiling of Ramses VI's tomb at Thebes; a sculpted head of Cleopatra could have been the double of the one I'd seen in the British Museum, and a bas relief that someone later told me depicted Hapi, the male god of the Nile who had the breasts of a woman because they were thought to represent fertility.

There were also some comfortable-looking chairs, an immense carved desk, and behind it stood Dr. Asfourh who could have lost 150 pounds and still been overweight. He was as fat as the late King Farouk I and even looked something like him, which he didn't seem to mind at all.

"You must be Mr. Padillo," Dr. Asfourh said in that rolling bass that to me sounded a little like spring thunder. "There's the Spanish in your eyes."

"The rest is Estonian," Padillo said, accepting Dr. Asfourh's hand. "This is my partner, Mr. McCorkle."

"Scot?" he said as he gave me his hand which was surprisingly small, but just as plump as I'd expected.

"Some," I said. "There's also some Irish and some English but it all goes back so far that nobody's really sure."

He spread his hands in an almost imploring manner. "Do sit down, gentlemen."

It took Dr. Asfourh a little while to seat himself because he did it cautiously, as if not too sure that the oversized executive chair was as sturdy as it looked. He grasped its arms firmly and then lowered himself into it slowly and carefully, but with a curious kind of dignity.

I guessed that he was somewhere between forty and forty-five. It's often hard to judge the age of those who are extremely fat. His head had turned itself into the shape of a big-bottomed pear because of the jowls that draped themselves from his chin line, almost obscuring his short neck, and making it seem difficult for him to smile because his mouth didn't like handling all that weight. But he smiled anyway—almost constantly—and I noticed that his teeth were white and even and probably capped. From the roundness of his face jutted a nose that was thin and sharp and beaked. It went with his dark, bitter eyes that flickered as they moved.

"I am Egyptian by birth, as you have probably gathered. But by choice I am an American citizen." He paused a moment as if brooding about that choice. "So. You are from Washington and you are here for what purpose—business or pleasure?"

"Mostly business," Padillo said. "Mr. McCorkle and I have a restaurant in Washington."

"Really? I have been in Washington on numerous occasions. What is it called?"

"Mac's Place," I said.

"Just off Connecticut?"

"That's right," Padillo said.

"Although I have not dined there, it was recommended to me. I do believe that the person who told me of it described it as superb. Is that true?"

"It's better than most," Padillo said. "Superb is a word that should be carefully used when it comes to restaurants."

Dr. Asfourh nodded his agreement as he smoothed a few long strands of black hair. He was nearly bald and the hair that was left grew just above his ears and formed several long thin arches over his white scalp. It didn't help much, I thought. He still looked bald.

"So. You are in San Francisco for what—a new chef? Perhaps a new maitre d'?" He didn't give us a chance to answer because he furnished his own. "No, you would be looking for neither at the Arabian Knight. It is not, as you may have noticed, a first-class joint." He smiled contentedly at his use of the phrase.

"We're thinking of expanding," Padillo said. "We've already looked into New York and Chicago. Now we're considering L.A. and San Francisco."

"All restaurant towns," Dr. Asfourh said, nodding his agreement again. "However, I am still at a loss as to why you're here. Jack's or Ernie's would seem far more suitable."

"We're also looking for a friend," I said.

"A friend?"

"He's from the Middle East. From Llaquah."

"Your restaurant was recommended to us as being a kind of informal headquarters for those from the Middle East," Padillo said.

"From Llaquah," Dr. Asfourh said. "Very few who come here are from Llaquah. But if they do, they always seem to be in transit. And they always want something. A free meal perhaps. A place to sleep. Even," he said, looking at us carefully, "even sometimes a place to hide."

"Do you provide that?" Padillo said.

Dr. Asfourh took a long cigar from the humidor on his desk and lit it carefully with a wooden match. "I have not always been a restaurant owner. In Alexandria I was a physician. A dedicated one, I might add. Perhaps too dedicated. I was forced to leave my country and emigrate to yours where I hoped to resume the practice of medicine. I then still entertained most of the ideas of my profession.

Dedication again. However, because of some incredible stupidity on the part of my colleagues in the American Medical Association, I was not permitted to practice in the United States unless I undertook a long, tedious and fruitless training program. Am I boring you?"

"Not at all," I said.

"To shorten my story, I refused to undergo the training and became an illicit abortionist. They were probably the happiest—and most profitable—years of my life." He paused as if to think about them. Fondly. "My dedication sloughed away as my bank account grew. Now, at the behest of the local authorities, I have retired from all practice. I pass the time operating this place and coming to the aid of those from the Arab world who find themselves in San Francisco—and in trouble."

"And you do all this out of compassion?" Padillo said.

Dr. Asfourh shook his head in what he may have hoped was a regretful manner. "I am afraid not, sir. As my dedication to humanity sloughed away it was replaced by other drives. Far simpler ones. Greed. And," he said, patting his enormous belly, "gluttony. Now the services I render my kinsmen I render only for money."

"Have you rendered any this evening to a short, plump, bald man from Llaquah?" Padillo said.

The doctor sighed. "It is difficult to remember."

Padillo took out his wallet and laid it on the edge of the desk.

"It gets easier," Asfourh said.

"How much?"

One fat hand moved in a small circle. "I will pique your curiosity first. It tends to create generosity. He was accompanied by an Englishman, a tall, thin chap."

"Go on," I said.

"They needed a place of safety for the night. And part of the morning. I think that much should be worth a trifle."

"How much is a trifle?" Padillo said.

"Shall we say a hundred?"

"Fifty."

"Very well, fifty."

Padillo pulled a fifty-dollar bill from his wallet and slid it across the smooth surface of the desk. The doctor looked at it and smiled happily.

"I gave them an address. For a price, of course."

Padillo nodded. "What's your price to give it to us?"

"Five hundred."

"Two."

"Perhaps four," the doctor said.

"Three."

Asfourh sighed. "I do so dislike haggling. Especially with women. That's the only phase of being an abortionist that was distasteful. Three fifty."

"Three twenty-five," Padillo said.

The doctor closed his eyes and nodded. Padillo took three hundreds, a twenty, and a five from the wallet and waved them gently back and forth. The doctor opened his eyes and smiled at them. One hand started toward the bills, but Padillo said, "The address first."

"Of course. It's a bit south of here on Mina Street. Should I write it down for you?"

"I'd like that," Padillo said. "You might also sign your name to it."

The doctor shrugged, opened his desk drawer,

took out a small, thick sheet of cream-colored paper, wrote the address, signed his name, and then smiled faintly as if he liked the look of his signature. He held out both hands, one to extend the paper and the other to receive the money. Padillo handed me the address as the doctor picked up the fifty-dollar bill from his desk, joined it to the other bills, and put them away in a pocket of his dark suit. He smiled again as if the feel of money made him happy.

Padillo and I rose and started to turn when the doctor cleared his throat as though there was something else that he would like to say, but wasn't quite sure how to bring it up.

He looked at Padillo and then at me and then back at Padillo.

"I sold that information cheaply, gentlemen, very cheaply, indeed."

"I don't think it was cheap," Padillo said.

"Demand always drives up the price."

"What demand?"

The doctor clasped his hands comfortably across his belly. "That in itself seems to be worth something, don't you think?"

"How much?"

"A hundred," he said. "And this time, no haggling."

Padillo turned to me. "Have you got it?"

"Barely."

"Pay him."

I took two fifties from my billfold and laid them on the desk. The doctor eyed them fondly.

"What demand?" Padillo said, his tone edged with harshness.

"Not fifteen minutes before you arrived, two

other gentlemen were here inquiring about the mysterious stranger from Llaquah."

"Did you give them the address?" I said.

"Of course not, Mr. McCorkle." He paused to smile. "I sold it to them for five hundred dollars. They didn't haggle at all."

Chapter 21

The address that Asfourh had given us was between Fifteenth and Sixteenth on Mina, a street that would have been an alley in any other town and didn't go much of any place in San Francisco. It was a small grim street with small grim two-story houses and I had the feeling that small grim people lived in them.

Somebody chose white the last time the houses were painted, but it had been a cheap job and now the paint was going, the victim of weather, city grime, and what I assumed to be collective indifference.

The houses were built nearly alike with small bay windows. Some of the windows displayed discouraged-looking potted plants. Others had been turned into pathetic shrines that featured tinted terra-cotta statues of Jesus, Mary, and assorted saints. And some of the windows offered nothing but shades that were drawn all the way down. The house that we were looking for was one of these.

Padillo and Wanda Gothar stared at it carefully as I drove past it toward Sixteenth.

"Chicano," Padillo said.

"The neighborhood?"

"This street anyway."

"I thought nice folks called them Mexican-Americans."

"Nice folks might," he said, "but us Chicanos don't."

"Ah. You're going to try to pass."

"Something like that," he said. "Go around the block and see how close you can park to that house."

I parked on the sidewalk next to a no parking sign three houses down. The sidewalk was where everyone else in that block parked. I turned and watched Padillo take off his necktie and unfasten three of his shirt buttons. "You have any lipstick?" he asked Wanda.

"Of course," Wanda said.

"Put it on. A lot of it. Mess up your hair, too. Look sloppy." He turned to me. "Loosen your tie and look a little drunk. In fact, we're all going to seem a little drunk. The Mex and his two gringo friends."

"It so happens that I have the remains of a pint here which might lend a little verisimilitude."

"Pass it around," Padillo said, taking his automatic from his waistband and checking it quickly.

I took the pint from beneath the seat, uncorked it, and handed it to Wanda. She took a drink and passed it to Padillo who drank deeply and then poured some of the whisky into his palm and rubbed it on his lapels. He handed the bottle to me and since there wasn't much left, only three or four swallows, I finished it off and felt some better. Not much, but some.

"You really think Kassim and Scales are still alive in there if Kragstein had a fifteen-minute lead on us?" Wanda said, running her hands through her pale blond hair, mussing it in vain, I thought, because she still looked pretty. Perhaps even beautiful.

"Do you have any better ideas?" Padillo said.

Wanda carefully applied some pale pink lipstick with three sure strokes. "You could tell me why you don't think Kragstein and Gitner killed my brother."

"When you come out of that house, you may know."

She turned to look at him. "You're still not sure, are you?"

"I've learned to trust my instincts."

"Is there anything else you trust?"

"Sure," Padillo said, "my feelings."

"Strange," she said. "I didn't think you had any."

It looked as if it might go on for the rest of the night, so I said, "It's getting late. If it's going to be done, let's do it."

"All right," Padillo said. "I'm the Mex pimp. I'm looking for a room where the three of us can have fun."

Wanda swore in German. I thought she did it quite well. Padillo ignored her. "Both of you just follow my lead. If they don't want to let us in, we go in anyway, so keep whatever you're shooting with handy."

"It's not what I'd call a carefully laid plan," Wanda said.

Padillo grinned at her. "Yet there's much to be said for the rewarding freshness of improvisation."

"Oh, Christ," I said, "let's go."

The house had no front yard. It was flush with the sidewalk and its bay window bellied out over it for a foot or so. The door was to the left of the window at the top of three wooden steps. Padillo slouched toward it and I followed, a little unsteadily, my left arm around Wanda who clutched her purse to her breasts, one hand inside of it, her finger probably on the trigger of the Walther PPK.

Padillo was leaning toward the door, his left palm resting on its jamb. He banged on it with his right fist. When no one answered, he banged again and in Spanish yelled for the crazy goats to open the door.

That got a response. The door opened about ten inches and a sleek young male head with a welter of long black, carefully combed hair popped out and yelled at Padillo to shut up. Padillo became all charm. He could do that when he wanted to. This time his charm was a little tipsy, but it was still there. In quick, idiomatic Spanish accompanied by a number of leers and gestures, he described what he wanted—a room where he and the two gringos could have fun. The young man with the long black hair looked at us with distaste. I nibbled Wanda Gothar's right ear. She smiled at the young man. He seemed to want no part of us until Padillo started to wave a twenty-dollar bill under his nose. The young man looked at us again, grimaced, shrugged, said something to Padillo in Spanish that I didn't catch, and then jerked his head toward the interior of the house.

Padillo started to go in first, but the young man blocked his entrance until the twenty-dollar bill changed hands. We followed Padillo into a hall. To the right was the living room with its bay window. The young man waved his hand toward it and told Padillo, "Go in there and wait. Someone will come to attend you."

"How long, friend?" Padillo said.

"Only a few minutes."

"That could be a long wait without something to drink."

"It will cost extra."

"The large foolish fat one will pay."

They were speaking Spanish, but it was simple enough for me to follow and I saw no cause for Padillo to be quite so graphic. He turned to me and said in a carefully accented voice, "We will all have a leetle drink, no? But it will cost."

"How much, pal?"

He shrugged. "Ten dollar."

"We oughta have a hell of a lot of little drinks for that," I said, but fumbled in my pocket, took out a crumpled wad of bills, and extricated a ten with all the careful concentration of a drunk. Padillo took it and handed it to the young man who tucked it away in a pocket of his tightfitting bell-bottomed black jeans. He wore a white nylon see-through shirt that was open to the waist so we could all admire the coiled rattlesnake that was tattooed on his hairless chest. He was all of nineteen and cute as a young scorpion.

The living room wasn't much. A large, color TV set was the principal attraction surrounded by a miscellany of furniture, most of it worn. There was a round oak table with four chairs at the end of the room near a door which led into the kitchen. We sat at the table.

"I'm going to argue with whoever comes in," Padillo said. "I'm going to insist on seeing the young punk again. When they both come back, we take them."

I nodded at him. Wanda Gothar didn't nod nor

did she say anything. She merely sat at the table, the purse on her lap, staring at the door and looking a little impatient and a little prim, as if wondering why the tea were late.

They came in fast, quite fast, the slim young one with the tattooed chest and the other one, bigger, older, and mean-looking. They separated quickly; the young one remained by the door and the other one, the mean-looking one, almost sprinted across the room. We didn't move, primarily because of the revolvers that each of them pointed at us. We stared at the two men and they stared back. The younger one with the see-through shirt started to say something, perhaps Put your hands up or Keep them where they are, but he never got it out because Wanda Gothar shot him in the chest, right through the head of the tattooed rattlesnake.

The man with the mean look turned to stare at the younger one. He had an opportunity to note the surprise that flitted across the young man's face before pain moved in, twisting the features into a caricature of agony that stayed there as he crumpled to the floor.

The older man started to turn back toward us, but Padillo was already across the room. His automatic slashed at the man's right wrist and the man's revolver flew away and I remember hoping that it wouldn't go off when it landed. The man yelled and grabbed his wrist and started to look around wildly, but then decided that there was nothing half so interesting as the automatic that Padillo held three inches away from his nose. The man had to cross his eyes to focus on it.

I looked back at the young man on the floor and the agony had gone from his face. He looked relaxed now. Relaxed and dead. Wanda Gothar wasn't looking at him. Instead, she examined the hole that she had shot through her purse. It wasn't a big hole and she seemed to be wondering whether she could have it repaired.

"Where are they?" Padillo asked, and when the mean-looking man said, "*No comprende,*" Padillo lifted the man's heavy chin with the slide end of his automatic so that the man had nothing to look at but the ceiling. Padillo switched to Spanish and in twenty-five words or less told the man what was going to happen to him unless he spoke truly. Most of Padillo's Spanish threat went far too fast for me, but what little I got didn't sound pleasant.

The man nodded, or tried to, but the automatic got in the way. Padillo lowered it and the man brought his head down, glanced once at the dead body on the floor, and said, "Okay. Okay. It's no skin off my ass." He spoke without accent.

"Where are they?" Padillo said again.

"They ain't here."

"Were they?"

The man nodded. "You mean the fat bald young guy and the tall skinny one?"

"That's right."

"They were here. Doc Asfourh sent them over and me and the kid were supposed to look after them till morning. It was just a one-night deal, you know."

"What happened?"

"Nothing happened. They stayed here for maybe thirty or forty-five minutes and then they left."

"Just like that?" Padillo said.

The man decided to rub the right wrist that Padillo's automatic had slashed. "Just like that," he said. He wasn't a very good liar.

"Does your wrist hurt?" Padillo said.

"Damn right it hurts."

"You want your other one to hurt?"

The man shook his head.

"What's your name?"

"Valdez. José Valdez."

"Bullshit," Padillo said.

The man shrugged. "Rogelio Quesada."

"All right, Señor Quesada. Let's hear it all."

The man glanced around the room again. He had deep-set narrow eyes and unless he opened them wide not much white showed. Above the eyes was a scant inch or so of forehead and below them was a spreadout nose and a mouth that snarled when it spoke and sneered when it didn't. He looked ugly and mean and big enough to back up his looks.

"What the hell am I gonna do with him?" he said, staring at the dead body.

"Call the cops," I said.

"Shit," he said.

"From the beginning," Padillo said.

Quesada tore his eyes from the body and sent them darting around the room again as if searching for the secret passage that would open up and let him through so that he could make it to San Diego by dawn. When he didn't find it he let his eyes settle on Padillo and snarled as he spoke. "Ah, Christ, it's no skin off my ass."

"You said that."

"Well, I get this call from Doc Asfourh and he wants to know if we've got something going and I tell him no so he says he wants to send a couple of creeps over who need a hidey hole till tomorrow morning. So I say how much and he says this much and I say it's not enough so we jew around with each other until we make a price. So these two creeps come over about fifteen minutes later and the kid and I send them upstairs and forget about them." He stopped talking and carefully started to pat his trouser pockets. "You gotta cigarette?" he asked Padillo.

"Give him a cigarette," Padillo said to me. I lit one and moved over to Quesada to hand it to him. He took it, inhaled mightily, blew out the smoke, and shrugged. "What the hell," he said.

"Go on," Padillo said."You've got them upstairs."

"Yeah, well, they're upstairs and being quiet and the kid and I are just fooling around down here when Doc Asfourh calls again. It was maybe fifteen, twenty minutes after they got here and the Doc says that two more guys are coming over and that they wanta see the two who're already here and for us to let 'em." He shrugged again. "So we did."

"Then what?"

"Then they got here—"

"What did they look like?" Padillo said.

"One was maybe fifty or so and had some whiskers. The other one was younger. They both looked like they knew their way around, if you know what I mean."

"Go on," Padillo said.

"Well, they asked where the other two was and I told them and they went upstairs and stayed maybe ten minutes. I wasn't paying no attention. It coulda been fifteen. Then all four of them come down and leave. Just like that."

"No guns?" Padillo said.

Quesada shook his head. "No guns. I wouldn't say they was all buddy-buddy, but I didn't see no guns."

"Then Asfourh called again," Padillo said.

Quesada nodded. "Uh-huh. He called again. He said that you three would be dropping around and that if me and the kid could keep you company until ten o'clock tomorrow morning there'd be a couple of bills in it for us. Well, what the hell. So look what happened. I don't think you had to go and shoot the kid. You didn't have no cause to go and do that."

"We'll call it an accident if it makes you feel any better," Padillo said.

Quesada again stared at the dead man on the floor. "You can call it anything you want to, but it ain't gonna make him feel any better."

"Did they say anything before they left?" Padillo said.

"No," Quesada said quickly, perhaps too quickly.

"Think hard."

"I'm thinking."

"Would fifty make it any easier?"

Quesada's face seemed to brighten. Or perhaps it was just greed. "Fifty wouldn't do much good, but a hundred would."

Padillo glanced at me and I shook my head. "I'm tapped out unless he'll take a credit card."

"Point something at him," Padillo said. I took the office .38 out of my coat pocket and pointed it at Quesada while Padillo got two fifties out of his bill-fold. There didn't seem to be much left. He handed the bills to Quesada who folded them into a small square which he tucked into his trousers' watch-pocket.

"Well, I wasn't paying much attention, y'unnerstand, because it wasn't none of my business."

"What did you hear that was none of your business?"

"Well, I heard the older guy, the one with the beard, you know, I heard him say something about the Criterion."

"What's the Criterion?"

"It used to be a picture show but it's not anymore. But that's still what they call the office building that it used to be in."

Padillo glanced at me. "You know where it is?"

I nodded. "It's south of Market. Skid row territory."

"That would suit Kragstein." He turned back to Quesada. "You said he said 'something' about the Criterion. What was the 'something'?"

"Christ, I don't know. I think the younger guy said where to now and the older guy, the one with the beard, said the Criterion and then I quit listening. I didn't give a shit."

Padillo half turned toward me and Wanda Gothar who still sat at the round table, her purse on her lap, looking totally uninterested in what was going on around her. "Let's go," he said.

She rose and started toward the door. I followed. When I was nearly there, Quesada said, "Hey." I turned as did Padillo.

"What?" I said.

Quesada jerked his thumb at the body of the dead youth. "Why don't you guys take him with you since you shot him and all?"

"No, thanks," I said.

"What the Christ am I supposed to do with him?"

"You'll think of something."

Quesada moved over to the body and squatted down beside it. He seemed to have forgotten us. He poked the dead man's shoulder, as if hoping that he were only asleep. "Why couldn't you go and get killed somewheres else," he said to the dead man. Then he looked up at us. "Why couldn't he, huh?"

"I don't really know," I said.

Chapter 22

The old Criterion Theater was located near Fifth and Howard in the heart of the area that countless winos and derelicts had shuffled through in their aimless pursuit of oblivion. I noticed that a lot of the old buildings had been torn down and if you liked to look at parking lots, you might say that the neighborhood had been improved.

The Criterion long ago had showed its last fourth-run double feature and now its marquee spelled out its latest attraction in carelessly spaced black letters which read, "Crists Own Home Gospil Mission Open 6 A.M." Whoever operated the mission either couldn't spell too well or couldn't locate the needed letters or just didn't think that it mattered. It probably didn't.

The Criterion Building itself was a seven-story brick affair that looked as if it had a long overdue date with the wrecker's ball. There seemed to be nothing about it either architecturally or historically that would cause anyone to protest its demolition. It was one of those buildings that cities tear down every day and when you pass by after they're gone you have to think hard to recall what had once been there.

The three of us sat at a table in the window of a cheap bar and grill across from the building and stared at it as we drank some suspicious-tasting Scotch. It was half past ten and I wondered who was working late in the lighted offices on the third and seventh floors and whether they were making any money.

"I didn't learn anything back there," Wanda Gothar said to Padillo. "I still think Gitner and Kragstein killed my brother."

"Think what you like," Padillo said.

"Who else could have?"

"McCorkle," Padillo said, not smiling.

She almost smiled, but not quite. "Not McCorkle. Not with a garrote. He'd get the ends confused and then say to hell with it and go back to the kitchen for a drink."

"That eliminates McCorkle. What about the people I used to work for? You remember Burmser. He didn't have much use for your brother. But more important was that the king wouldn't have anything to do with official protection. So Burmser has your brother killed in McCorkle's apartment and then pressures me into signing on. That gives him a man on the scene."

"That seems a little farfetched," I said. "Even for Burmser."

"I guess it does," Padillo said.

"Well, what about the king and Scales?" I said. "They may be a little short on motive and opportunity, but if we put our minds to it, we could probably work something out."

They both ignored me as Wanda Gothar took a sip of her Scotch, shuddered slightly, and said, "So whom does that leave?"

"It leaves you, Wanda," Padillo said.

"You're forgetting Kragstein and Gitner again."

"Your motive's just as good. You're also one of the few people who Walter would let get behind him.

With him out of the way, you'd get the entire pie, not just half. Then you could hire me—or someone like me—for nickels and dimes. It's the perfect motive. Money."

"You're forgetting my alibi."

"The 'high Government official' you were shacked up with while Walter was getting himself killed?" Padillo made his voice put "high Government official" in quotes. "Maybe he'd been at the track too often and was down on his luck. He'd give you an alibi for a price."

She looked at me. "Where does he get them?"

"From a wholesaler," I said.

"There's only one thing wrong with your theory, Padillo," she said.

"What?"

"I wouldn't kill Walter and you know it."

He nodded. "There's that."

"I still think it was Kragstein and Gitner."

"There's one way to find out."

"What?" she said.

He nodded toward the Criterion Building. "You can go ask them."

"That's what you've had in mind all along, isn't it?"

"Why don't we just wait for them to come out?" I said. "The king and Scales ran out on us. Maybe they've hired some new babysitters—Kragstein and Gitner. Maybe nobody wants them dead anymore. Maybe all four of them are sitting up there right now playing dominoes and chuckling about how dumb we are."

"You think it's all been dumb, don't you, Mac?" Padillo said.

"Not dumb. Just less than brilliant."

He nodded. "I can't argue with that. But I'll go in there, knowing it's dumb, because I have to find Gitner and because once he leaves that building, my chances of finding him again will be next to nothing. Wanda's going because of her brother. You don't have any reason to go and if you want to sit here and drink your Scotch until it's over, nobody's going to object."

"You make a nice little talk," I said.

Padillo turned to Wanda. "That means he's going with us."

She shook her head slightly as if puzzled. First she looked at me and then at Padillo. "Why?"

Padillo shrugged. "Ask him."

She looked at me again. "Why?" she said and there was real wonder in her voice.

"I don't like to feel left out," I said.

The lock on the front door of the Criterion Building was broken. It could have been broken that night or the month before and I bet myself it would stay broken until they tore down the building which didn't look as if it contained much worth stealing anyway.

The lobby had a white tile floor with some black tiles that spelled out Criterion Building and it probably had looked neat and businesslike back in 1912, but now the titles were a dirty gray and some of them were chipped and broken and a lot more were missing.

The two elevators wore OUT OF ORDER signs that looked almost as old as the building. To the left was a cigar stand, its glass case empty, its shelves bare. A man was curled up behind the case asleep, a half-empty wine bottle clutched to his chest.

"We walk," Padillo said.

"There were lights on the third and seventh floors," Wanda said.

We stopped at the building directory. The overhead light for the lobby was out—permanently, it seemed—and someone had rigged up an extension cord with a forty-watt bulb that dangled over the building directory. The second and third floors still had some occupants—a novelty company, a manufacturer's representative, a collection agency, all last-gasp businesses with no need for much of a front nor the ability to pay for one. There were no occupants listed for any floor above the fourth.

"I'll bet on seven," I said.

"We'll check out three first," Padillo said. "Kragstein may be having one of his clever nights."

At the third-floor landing Padillo, his gun drawn, opened the door cautiously to peer down the corridor. He opened it wide and slipped through. Wanda and I followed. She held the Walther in her right hand, her purse in her left. I decided to take the thirty-eight out of my jacket pocket.

The light that we'd seen from downstairs came from an office at the far end of the corridor. We tiptoed toward it, skirting a broken desk, three old wooden file cabinets, and a collection of mismatched office chairs that some former tenant had moved as far as the corridor before he said to hell with it.

The lighted door was half frosted glass and half wood. Carefully lettered in black on the glass was "The Arbitrator, Miss Nancy deChant Orumber, Editor." Padillo motioned us to the other side of the door where we flattened ourselves against the wall. He took up a similar position next to the door knob, reached for it, turned it, and flung the door open. It banged against something inside the office. We waited, but nothing happened. We waited some more and then a woman's voice asked in a cool, polite tone, "May I help you?"

She wore a gray leghorn hat with a wide brim and a narrow white band that had some artificial flowers attached to it. Pink roses, I think. She sat behind an old but carefully polished oak desk which was covered with what seemed to be galley proofs. Two sides of the room were lined with bookshelves that contained bound copies that had *The Arbitrator* lettered on them in gold ink and below that the year of their issue. They went all the way back to 1905.

She looked at us with unwavering bright blue eyes that were covered with gold-rimmed spectacles. Her hair was white and she held a fat black editor's pencil in her right hand. Next to her on a stand was an L. C. Smith typewriter. There was a black phone on the desk and against the outer wall were three cabinets that the door had banged against. Everything was spotlessly clean.

She asked again if she could help us and Padillo hastily stuck his automatic back in his waistband and said, "Security, ma'am. Just checking."

"This building hasn't had a night watchman since nineteen-sixty-three," she said. "I do not think you are telling the truth, young man. However, you seem too well dressed to be bandits, especially the young lady. I like your frock, my dear."

"Thank you," Wanda said.

"I am Miss Orumber and this is my last night in this office so I welcome your company although I must say that well brought up young ladies and gentlemen are taught to knock before entering. You will join me in a glass of wine, of course."

"Well, I don't think that—" Padillo didn't get the chance to finish.

"Nonsense," she said, rising and moving over to one of the filing cabinets. "There was a time when we would have had champagne, but—" She let her sentence trail off as she brought out a bottle of sherry, placed it on the desk, returned to the file cabinet, and produced four long-stemmed wine-glasses which she polished with a clean white cloth.

"You, young man," she said to me. "You look as though you may have acquired a few of the social graces along the way. There's character in your face. Some would probably call it dissipation, but I choose to call it character. You may pour the wine."

I looked at Padillo who shrugged slightly. I poured the wine and handed glasses all around.

"We will not drink to me," she said, "but to *The Arbitrator* and to its overdue demise. *The Arbitrator.*" We sipped the wine.

"In nineteen-twenty-one a man sent me a Pierce-Arrow. A limousine. The only condition was that I include his name in that year's edition of *The Arbitrator.* A limousine, can you imagine? No gentleman would present a lady with a limousine unless he also provided a chauffeur. The man was a boor. Needless to say his name was not included."

She had a lined, haughty face with a thin nose and a still strong chin. She could have been a beauty fifty or sixty years ago, one of those tall imperious types that Gibson once drew.

"What is *The Arbitrator,*" Padillo asked, "San Francisco's social register?" I think he was trying to be polite.

"Not is, young man, but was. It ruled San Francisco society for nearly forty years. I have been its only editor. Now society in San Francisco is no more and after this edition, neither is *The Arbitrator.*"

She finished her drink in quick, tiny sips. "I shan't keep you," she said, moving around her desk and lowering herself into the chair. "Thank you for coming."

We turned to go, but she said, "Do you know something? Today is my birthday. I had quite forgotten. I am eighty-five."

"Our best wishes," I said.

"I've edited *The Arbitrator* since nineteen-o-nine. This will be the last edition, but I said that, didn't I? May I ask you something, young man? You with the brooding eyes," she said, nodding at Padillo.

"Anything," he said.

"Can you think of a more ridiculous way to spend a lifetime than deciding who should or should not be considered members of something called society?"

"I can think of several," he said.

"Really? Do tell me one to cheer me up."

"I'd hate to spend a lifetime worrying about whether I belonged to something called society."

She brightened. "And the bastards did worry, didn't they?"

"Yes," Padillo said. "I'm sure they did."

We started moving up the stairs again, checking each floor as we went. There was nothing on any of them but dust and dirt and discarded furniture.

We stopped before taking the stairs that led to the seventh floor. Padillo turned to look at Wanda and me. "I don't think we're going to be much of a surprise," he said.

"It's a set-up?" I asked.

"When Kragstein dropped the name of this building," Wanda said, "he didn't drop it casually."

"Well?" Padillo said.

"Let's go," I said. He looked at Wanda. After a moment she nodded.

"I'll take the center of the corridor," he said. "McCorkle will take the right." He glanced at Wanda. "You take the left. If something happens, dive in the nearest office. If not, we'll bust into the office with lights just like we did before."

The seventh-floor corridor was much the same as the others. There was dust and some untidy piles of abandoned office forms. Two scarred desks on broken legs tilted toward each other. Next to them was an old-fashioned water cooler minus its glass bottle. Light shone through the frosted pane of a closed door toward the end of the corridor.

We moved slowly, checking each office. They were all empty. Once more we took up positions flat against the wall on each side of the lighted door. Padillo turned the knob and gave the door a hard shove. It swung in, banging against the wall. Padillo crouched as he darted in, his automatic extended like a fat steel forefinger. I followed, going in low and fast and then scuttling crablike to my left. I needn't have bothered. There was nothing in the office but the king and Scales.

They were seated on the floor leaning against the right wall. Their legs were tied at the ankles with what appeared to be steel wire. Their arms were behind them, apparently bound at the wrists. Broad strips of white surgical tape were plastered across their mouths. Their eyes were as wide as they could get them.

Wanda Gothar stood next to me as Padillo moved over to the king and reached for the strip of surgical tape. He grasped one end and gave it a hard yank. The king yelled. A voice behind me said, "Don't turn, Padillo."

He turned anyway, his move incredibly fast, but it wasn't any use. Something had jammed itself into my right kidney. Padillo stopped his turn, bent forward, and placed his automatic on the floor next to his right foot. He straightened and shrugged.

The voice behind me said, "I didn't think it would be so easy, Mike." It was Gitner's voice.

"There was a time he'd have tried for your legs," another voice said. I'd heard that one before, too. It was Kragstein's. "But that was a long time ago, wasn't it, Michael?" His voice came from behind and to my left. I assumed that Wanda Gothar had a gun in her kidneys, too. I didn't turn my head to look. "Slowly and carefully, McCorkle," Gitner said. "Bend down and put your gun on the floor, just like Padillo did."

"You do the same, Wanda," Kragstein said.

I did as I was told and when I straightened, Gitner said, "Turn slowly to your left, McCorkle. Very slowly. Walk over to the wall and lean against it, arms and legs apart, just like on TV."

"Padillo goes first," Kragstein said.

"All right, Padillo, move," Gitner said.

Padillo headed toward the wall opposite the king and Scales. He moved past my line of vision. I had nothing to look at now but the bound pair on the floor. The king smiled at me tentatively, but I didn't smile back. I didn't feel like it.

"All right, McCorkle. Your turn."

He prodded me over to the wall. Padillo and Wanda were already leaning against it. I assumed the position, something I'd never done before, and found that I didn't like it. Gitner ran his hands over me, but discovered nothing that he wanted.

"Why aren't they dead?" Padillo said.

"That should be obvious, old friend," Kragstein said. "They're far more valuable alive. We've come to an understanding."

"You get a cut of the five million, right?"

"Let's just say that under the new arrangement we now work for the king."

"There's nothing new about that," Padillo said.

"I don't follow you, old friend."

"I may be getting slow, Kragstein, but you're getting dumb. You've always worked for the king. You just didn't know it."

Chapter 23

There was a silence that lasted for nearly fifteen seconds until the king made a noise that began as a scornful laugh but ended as a nervous titter.

"Turn around, Padillo," Kragstein said, his voice sounding strained and tight. "Keep your hands behind you."

I sensed rather than saw Padillo straighten and turn. "Like this?" he said.

"Like that," Kragstein said. "Now let's have that remark again."

"About how dumb you're getting?"

It sounded like a slap. A hard one. "Your wit has always bored me," Kragstein said. "You've got ten seconds to explain it."

"It'll take longer than that," Padillo said.

"Take the tape of Scales's mouth and undo their hands," Kragstein said and I assumed he was talking to Gitner. There was a brief silence and then I heard the tape being ripped off. Scales didn't yell.

"All right, Padillo, start," Kragstein said.

"Who approached you?" Padillo said. "Somebody we both know in England?"

"Who told you?"

"Scales. He didn't tell me really. He said that somebody who had once been in British Intelligence recommended me. Now who could that be?"

"Clegg," Kragstein said, breathing the name out.

"Harold Clegg," Padillo said. "He also recommended the Gothars, according to Scales. How did Harold look when he approached you, Kragstein? Well, I hope."

"It doesn't make sense," Gitner said. "Why would they hire somebody to bodyguard them and then turn around and hire somebody to try to kill them?"

"Nobody ever said you had brains, Gitner, but I've always credited Kragstein with some."

Kragstein forgot to hit Padillo again. I heard someone walk across the room. When Kragstein spoke again, his voice sounded farther away. He said only one word: "Talk."

"He's raving." Scales said. "Padillo's angry because his incompetence frightened his Majesty and forced us to seek refuge elsewhere. He's obviously trying to save his own—" A hard slap interrupted Scales. He whimpered a little.

"Talk," Kragstein said again.

"I'm telling you the truth," Scales insisted. His voice broke on the last word and rose to a high falsetto.

"He says you're lying, Padillo," Kragstein said.

"You didn't hit him hard enough. Try the king."

"Don't hit me!" the king said. He sounded frightened.

"It will be far worse than a simple blow, I'm afraid, if you don't talk. Now I'm going to ask some questions." Kragstein paused. "They can be answered with a yes or no. If I think that you're lying, I am going to hurt you. If you continue to lie, I am going to hurt you very bad. Is that clear?"

"Yes," the king said, "it's clear."

"Did Harold Clegg recommend the Gothars and

suggest that you retain my services? And did Clegg also recommend Padillo?"

"I didn't retain anyone," the king said in a whisper so low that I could barely hear it. "I don't know any Harold Clegg."

"Did Scales?"

"I don't know."

There was a thud or a thump that was followed by a high-pitched scream. I assumed that Kragstein had kicked the king. "I don't know!" he screamed.

"It was Clegg," Scales said in a dull, resigned tone. "He recommended the Gothars and also Padillo. I used another intermediary to get him to recommend you, but Clegg didn't know it."

"It's pretty, isn't it?" Padillo said. "We've all been working for the same boss. You've been trying to kill him and we've been trying to keep him from getting killed and he picks up the tab for both operations."

"I had nothing to do with it," the king said. "Nothing."

"Not much," Padillo said. "How large a slice of the five million did they offer you, twenty percent?"

"Ten," Kragstein said.

"That's because they didn't need us anymore. But even if they didn't need us, there was still the chance that you'd kill them. So they decided to buy you off. It could have worked if the king weren't such a rotten actor. Why do you think they really hired you, Kragstein?"

"I still don't know that they did."

"Ask Scales. Ask him hard."

There was another thud that was followed by a moan. This time it must have been Scales who got kicked. I was growing tired of leaning spreadeagled against the wall so I started to shift my hands. Something dug into my kidney hard enough to hurt and Gitner said, "Don't."

"Why did you hire us through an intermediary, Scales?" Kragstein said.

The pain was evident in his voice, but nevertheless Scales tried to lie. He wasn't good at it and he seemed to know that he wasn't, but he tried anyway. "It was a mistake. I didn't—"

Kragstein didn't want to hear about any mistakes. "You tell it, Padillo. Your version."

"Fine," Padillo said. "Suppose you were visiting royalty who wanted to travel across the country incognito. First, you'd have to get the State Department off your back. Then you'd have to avoid representatives of your own country. So you hire yourself an assassin, an international hit man. Better yet, you hire yourself a pair of them through an intermediary. That gives you the reason for traveling incognito. But because you don't want to die, you also hire yourself a couple of topflight bodyguards and just to make sure that nothing's really going to happen to you, you make them hire a backup man—me. If Washington offers you official protection, you turn it down with the claim that you're convinced that it's either incompetent or because it can be corrupted—and you cite the deaths of the Kennedys and King to prove your point. How does it sound so far, Kragstein?"

"I'm still listening."

"It's a gamble, of course. You have to make the threat real. So you actually bet your life that the crowd you hired to protect you is better than the bunch that you hired to kill you. If you win, you win five million dollars."

There was a silence. Finally, Kragstein said, "When did you find out, Padillo?"

"It didn't come to me in a dream. The king kept making mistakes. Little ones. They began to add up."

There was another silence. I wanted to say something, to venture an incisive comment perhaps, but nobody asked what I thought. They probably didn't care.

The silence kept on growing until Kragstein said, "Who else knows?"

"Only one other person."

"Knows what, for Christ's sake?" Gitner said.

"Padillo's right, Gitner," Kragstein said. "You are dumb."

"Small words," Gitner said. "Use small words and maybe I'll understand. Only one other person knows what?"

I could hear Kragstein sigh. "That the king's not really a king. He's a ringer."

"Ah, shit," Gitner said.

"You said somebody else knows, Padillo. Who?"

"You don't have to worry about him."

"Why?"

"Because he's dead. Because the king killed him."

I caught her move. It was a bare, peripheral glance, but one moment Wanda Gothar was leaning against the wall next to me and a moment later she was gone and then there was a high-pitched scream. I could sense that Gitner had moved away so I turned around. She was trying to kill the king and she knew how to do it. Her right arm was around his neck and she had his head bent back at an almost impossible angle. The king flopped about on the floor, his hands clawing at Wanda's right arm.

I glanced at Padillo. He wasn't watching the battle. He was watching Gitner who wasn't watching the battle either. He had moved to the door and stood there in a slightly crouched stance, his revolver aimed at Padillo's stomach.

Kragstein moved in and aimed a hard, chopping blow at Wanda's neck. She rolled away from it and it probably saved the king's life because she loosened her hold and then lost it completely when Kragstein hit her again, aiming once more for her neck but catching the back of her ducked head.

She was up then and if her timing had been a little better, Kragstein would have been dead. Her left arm shot out, her knuckles clenched and extended. Kragstein ducked his chin, protecting his throat, and her blow smashed into his nose. The blood spurted once and then flowed down around Kragstein's mouth and into his beard.

She was good, very good, and I understood why she was in the business she was in. She could have escorted me to the bank anytime. But she weighed only 120 pounds to Kragstein's 180 or so and in fifty years he had learned a few nasty tricks which nobody had yet got around to teaching her.

He used one of them when he feinted a left at her head. It wasn't much of a feint and she caught his fist with both of her hands and her fingers dug for the nerve between his thumb and forefinger. But instead of pulling back, Kragstein went with the blow and I saw his right hand move. It moved only six inches or so, but he got his shoulder into it. She saw it coming and tried to turn her left hip to it while digging even harder at the nerve in his left hand. Kragstein yelled but managed not to pull his right and it smashed into her low and knocked her back against the wall where she bent over and gasping, sank to her knees, her hands pressed to her lower abdomen.

Kragstein glanced quickly at the king and Scales and then turned toward Padillo and me. He now had his revolver out again.

"She almost had you," Padillo said and smiled cheerfully.

"Almost," Kragstein said, mopping at his bloody beard with a handkerchief. "You knew she'd try it, didn't you?"

"Yes."

"But Gitner wasn't as dumb as you thought."

Padillo shrugged. "Being careful doesn't make him smart."

"Being smart is my department, isn't it?" He turned toward the king and Scales. The king was huddled up next to the wall, his hands clasped around the back of his neck. Scales was still seated, leaning against the wall, staring at nothing.

"Who is he?" Kragstein said to Scales.

Scales didn't look at the king. He still stared blankly at nothing. Or he could have been watching his dreams disintegrate. "An actor," he said. "An unemployed actor."

"He's from Llaquah?"

"Yes. I knew him there. Then he came to London. He wanted to be an actor. A second Omar Sharif. But he was not nearly good enough."

"What happened to the real king?"

"He sent for me you know. He really did. When he came out of the monastery, he sent for me. He said he needed me. I came over from London. We were going out to dinner the third night I was there and he was taking a shower in the flat that he had borrowed. He slipped and broke his neck. It was an accident. A foolish accident."

"What happened then?" Kragstein said.

"I buried him that night."

"Where?"

"In the Bois de Boulogne. The plan just came to me." He glanced at the king. I still thought of him as the king. I suppose I always will. "I remembered that there was a strong resemblance. And no one had seen the king during the five years that he was in the monastery. A man can change between sixteen and twenty-one. I had all the credentials. It seemed worth the chance."

"It still is," Kragstein said.

Scales looked up at him. Some life came back into his eyes. He didn't speak, but the question was on his face.

Kragstein nodded. "No one at the oil companies ever saw the real king?"

"As a child perhaps, but not as an adult."

"And you're sure nobody else knows?"

"No one," Scales said. "No one possibly could. Gothar was beginning to suspect. We made a slight slip. So we sent him a telegram, urging him to be at McCorkle's apartment. We signed Padillo's name to it." He began to talk faster, as if he found release in the confession. "When we arrived there, we told him that we'd also received a telegram. I handed it to him—we'd sent it to ourselves—and he—" Scales paused to look thoughtfully at the huddled figure of the king. "He went behind Gothar and used the garrote. I thought of the garrote. I thought that it might confuse things."

"Not bad," Kragstein said. "Not bad at all. Now then. What are the arrangements concerning the money?"

Scales shrugged. "The king's dead brother arranged it all. As soon as the papers are signed, the oil company deposits five million dollars to the king's account in Switzerland."

"Numbered?"

"Of course."

"That would give us about two days," Kragstein said.

Scales looked up at him again. "To do what?"

"To withdraw the money."

"You're going through with it, aren't you?" Padillo said.

Kragstein gave him a brief glance. "Of course. There's going to be a slight change, however."

"What change?" Scales asked.

"Your share will now be one million instead of four and a half million. Agreed?"

Scales hesitated only for a moment. "Agreed," he said.

"How about your buddy over there?" Gitner said.

"Ask him," Scales said.

"How about you, king?" Gitner said.

The king raised his head and looked at Gitner. "I no longer care," he said. "I should never have listened to him. Never."

"You should have also researched your role a little better," Padillo said.

"What did he do wrong?" Kragstein asked. He sounded quite interested.

"Prayers and fish," Padillo said. "He was supposed to be a devout Catholic. Anyone who'd spend five years in a monastery would be. I saw him pray once. He didn't cross himself. I don't think he knows how. In New York we had veal on Friday. He ate it. I don't care what the Vatican says, a really hard-nosed Catholic wouldn't and that's what he was supposed to be."

"That's thin, Padillo," Kragstein said.

"That just started me wondering," Padillo said. "When they ran out on us I became sure. If he'd been for real, he would have run to the police regardless of what he thought of them. When he didn't, he had to have something to hide. I was fairly sure I knew what it was."

"It sounds good now anyway," Gitner said.

"I don't think it matters a damn how it sounds," Padillo said. "What matters now is what happens next."

"To you," Kragstein said.

"That's right. To me."

"We'll have to think of something, won't we?"

Chapter 24

They made the king and Scales help Wanda walk down eight flights of stairs to the basement of the building. She threw up twice on the way. We stopped before a small room in the basement, not much more than eight by ten, that contained a desk and three chairs which looked as if they'd been salvaged from one of the abandoned offices upstairs.

The door to the room was made of steel and it had a metal bar with a hole in its end that could be swung down and padlocked into place so that nobody could get in. If somebody was inside and the bar was down, it wouldn't matter about the padlock. They couldn't get out.

The king and Scales helped Wanda into the room. They turned her around, pushed her into one of the chairs, and then backed off quickly, as if glad to be done with a distasteful chore. She was bent over from the waist, her hands clasped hard against her middle, her head almost touching her knees. She made no sound.

The room was lit with a weak bulb in a ceiling fixture. The king and Scales came out of the room and stood near Gitner. They looked uneasy, frightened, and—I thought—a little embarrassed. Kragstein moved into the room and over to Wanda. He shifted his revolver to his left hand and with his right grasped her pale blond hair and jerked her head up. She still made no sound. She simply stared at him with those cold blue eyes. If there were no tears in them, I thought I could see plenty of hate.

"What arrangements have you made?" Kragstein said.

She ran her tongue over her lips. "It's a full-dress affair. The boards of directors, their chairmen, the presidents of the companies. There'll also be assorted guests. Wives, I think. Other company officials."

"Reporters? TV?"

"No. But they'll have sound cameras. They're going to make a film on what the transaction will mean to Llaquah. The signing of the agreement will be part of it. I specified no press, but they may send out film clips later."

"When will they sign?"

"At ten tomorrow morning. Or this morning. On the twenty-ninth floor of the headquarters on Bush Street. They're to be there by nine thirty."

"Whom should they ask for?"

"Arnold Briggs. He's head of public relations."

"What security arrangements did you request?"

"I told them to make it tight. They'll probably use private detectives from one of the larger firms."

"That means Gitner and I can't get in."

"Scales could get you in."

Kragstein abruptly let go of her head and she dropped it back down near her knees and started to make small retching sounds.

Kragstein turned toward the door and motioned with his revolver. "Bring them in," he said to Gitner.

I moved before Gitner could prod me with his revolver again. Padillo followed and when we were in the room he looked around and selected a worn swivel chair to sit in. I took what was left—a golden oak thing that had one of its arms missing. Padillo tilted back in his chair and looked first at Gitner, then at Kragstein.

"When do you do it?" he said.

"Not now and not here," Kragstein said. "We don't want you to be found for a while."

Padillo nodded as if he considered Kragstein's reasoning sound. "It's a big bay," he said.

"That's what you would use, wouldn't you?"

"That's what I would use," Padillo said.

"Before or after it's signed?"

Padillo seemed to think about it. "Before."

Kragstein looked at his watch. "It's almost two now. We'll be coming for you around seven." He stood there as if waiting for Padillo to say something else. When he didn't, Kragstein backed from the room, preceded by Gitner. The king and Scales were murmuring to each other and shifting uneasily from one foot to another. When Gitner and Kragstein had backed from the room, one of them told the king and Scales to close the door. The king closed it slowly, staring at us as if trying to memorize what we looked like. Scales didn't look at us at all.

We heard the metal bar clang into place. I thought there was a curiously final note about its sound. Padillo swiveled his chair around to look at Wanda. She was still bent over, still clutching her stomach. She had stopped retching.

"How bad is it, Wanda?" Padillo said.

"Quite bad," she said without looking up. "Bending over like this seems to help."

"Did he rupture anything?"

"No," she said. "I don't think so."

"Can you listen?"

"I can listen."

And that's what we did for nearly half an hour while Padillo outlined one of his getaway plans that sounded like a sure thing if one or two of us didn't mind getting shot.

It took almost an hour to work the nail out of the desk. Padillo found it driven into one of the lower drawers. It had been used by someone who had grown tired of having the drawer come apart. Glue would have been better—more craftsmanlike—or even a small screw, but whoever had owned the desk hadn't wanted to bother with either so he had nailed the drawer together with the first one he could find—a three-inch finishing nail.

When we finally got it out, Padillo lit a match and held it to the nail. "Do you think this really does any good?" he asked me.

"I don't know, but everybody seems to do it."

"Here," he said, handing it to me. He bent down and rolled up his left trouser leg. I handed him back the nail and then Wanda Gothar and I watched as he drove it into the calf of his leg.

He drove it for almost half an inch, biting hard on his lip, the rest of his face screwed up into pain that mingled with determination. I couldn't have done it. He withdrew the nail and watched the wound bleed. For a puncture, it bled freely.

"All right, Wanda," he said.

Wanda Gothar lay down on the desk. I went around to the other side of it. Padillo swung his left leg up over Wanda so that his calf was just below her throat. I held his foot. The blood dripped on to Wanda's dress. We moved it around so that it dripped all over her front. She watched it for a while and then closed her eyes. When the puncture seemed to be coagulating, Padillo poked at it with the nail and it started to bleed again. After ten minutes or so he decided that there was enough blood.

He swung his leg back down, took out a handkerchief, and bound the puncture tightly. Wanda Gothar sat up and stared down at her bloodied dress. She shook her head and looked up and said, "Have either of you a cigarette?"

I handed her one and lit it. Then I offered one to Padillo, took one myself, and we sat there smoking silently until Wanda said, "What time is it?"

I looked at my watch. "Six thirty-five."

"How do you feel?" Padillo asked her.

"Better. Much better."

We had gone over it enough so that there was no reason to talk about it anymore. We sat there in silence, not looking at each other, not looking at anything, until we heard the metal bar being drawn. Wanda lay down on the desk. One arm dangled over its edge. Her head lolled back. She turned herself slightly on one side so that her blood-soaked front face the door. She looked as if someone had dumped her dead on the desk which is just how we wanted her to look.

The door opened and Kragstein stood there with his revolver drawn. Gitner was at his side. Kragstein looked at Wanda, then at us, then back at Wanda.

"What's wrong with her?" he said.

"You hit her too hard," I said. "She started hemorrhaging about two hours ago. We couldn't stop it. She's dead."

Kragstein didn't seem to care. "You'll have to carry her out," he said.

Padillo and I rose and went to opposite sides of the desk. Each of us put an arm under Wanda's knees and our other arm around her back. We picked her up. She made herself dead weight and let her head roll back. She was a good actress.

We carried her through the door. Kragstein was on our left pointing his revolver at Padillo. Gitner was on our right. Padillo murmured, "Now," and we hurled Wanda at Gitner. She landed on him kicking and clawing. I dived at his legs, slamming into them with my shoulder, bowling him over. Wanda was still on top of him when I came up in a roll. Gitner tried to slam her head with his revolver. I kicked his hand and the gun sailed across the room. I grabbed Wanda's arm and jerked her off Gitner. "Go," I yelled and shoved her toward the stairs. She stumbled, recovered, and darted toward them. I aimed another kick at Gitner, but he rolled away. I spotted a door that looked as if it led somewhere and ran toward it. I looked back once, Padillo was locked with Kragstein. I couldn't tell who was winning.

I went through the door, saw a narrow flight of stairs, and ran for them. I was halfway up when Gitner lunged for my left ankle, caught it, and gave it a hard yank. I fell forward and kicked back with my right leg. I hit something and my left ankle came free. I scrambled on up the stairs, puffing a bit now. Gitner was a few feet behind me. I doubt that he was puffing at all.

At the top of the stairs there was another door, a heavy, metal one. I pulled it open and went through. In front of me, across a wide expanse of wooden flooring, a sea of black and white faces stared at me. There was a podium with a man standing behind it, his back to me. He turned quickly when a few members of his audience pointed in my direction. When he raised his arms in benediction and called, "Welcome, Brother," I realized that I was onstage in the old Criterion Theater at the early morning session of Crists Own Home Gospil Misson.

I ran toward the man's welcome arms. But he was looking past me now. "You, too, Brother!" he called. "Jesus bids you welcome!"

I looked back. Gitner was racing across the stage at me. Some of the audience, those who were sober enough to see, gave a faint cheer. Gitner was grinning, as if he looked forward to what he was about to do.

Gitner was too good for me, Padillo had said. Too fast, too tricky. I backed into the man who had welcomed me. "Go away," I said and he said, "Right you are, Brother," and started moving stage left. Gitner wasn't running anymore. He moved toward me slowly, his arms and hands almost chest high, all ready to maim or kill, whichever seemed more promising. He grinned as he came. Then he stopped grinning and said. "This is gonna be fun."

I backed into the podium. I moved to my left. I risked a glance at the podium, hoping there would be a heavy pitcher of water. There wasn't. It contained only a large Bible. I snatched it up and threw it at Gitner and then dived in low after it, praying a little as I went.

His hands flew up to protect his face from the Bible and my head hit him hard just below the breastbone. It knocked him off balance, but not before he had brought his clenched hands down on my left shoulder. If he had hit my neck, he might have broken it. We fell and I landed on top of him and it was like landing on three wildcats. His left thumb found my right eye and he was digging into it and chopping at me with his right hand when I brought my knee up into his crotch. He screamed and I jumped up. He got up faster than he should, faster than anyone should, so I kicked him in the pit of the stomach. I kicked him hard and the audience yelled its approval. One man screamed, "Kill the son of a bitch!"

Gitner must have had a cast-iron stomach. He kept on coming. He even grinned a little. I aimed a left at his heart. It was a good left and I put everything I had into it. Gitner moved back half a step, turned sideways, caught my fist, pulled me over and down, and broke my arm.

I was on the floor looking up at him, looking up at death really, when Padillo landed on his back. There was nothing sportsmanlike about it. Padillo got his left forearm around Gitner's neck, dug a knee into his back, and with the heel of his palm under Gitner's nose forced his head back until the neck snapped. Gitner died on his way to the floor. The audience roared its delight.

Padillo looked down at Gitner and over at me. "You were out of your class."

"I wasn't doing too bad until he broke my arm."

Padillo shook his head. "You should have stuck to your original plan," he said as he helped me up.

"What?"

"You should have sat on him and squashed him flat."

Chapter 25

When the intern with the blond goatee at Emergency Hospital Central over on Polk Street asked, "What happened to you?" I thought a moment and then said, "I fell out of a tree."

Padillo and I had left the Criterion Theater stage hurriedly, going back down the stairs to the basement, past the sprawled body of Kragstein, and up another flight of stairs that led to an alley. As we had moved past Kragstein, I said. "He almost died rich."

"He died poor in a back alley hole in San Francisco. That's what happens when you stay in it too long."

"The smart ones get out?"

"The smart ones never get in."

We had caught a cab just as two squad cars spilled a load of uniformed and plainclothes police under the Criterion's marquee.

"Some wino got his," the cabdriver said wisely. "He probably got stabbed over a quarter."

"I heard it was a little more than that," I said.

Padillo had dropped me off at the hospital at 7:45. I only yelled once when the intern set my arm which he said had a "nice clean little fracture."

"It hurts like hell," I said.

"I'll give you some pills for the pain."

After he had enveloped my forearm with a cast, he gave me a small white envelope that said, "One every fours hours if pain persists." I looked inside. There were four white pills. I swallowed them all, but the pain persisted.

At 9:15 Padillo returned to the hospital carrying a large oblong cardboard box under his arm. "How bad is it?" he said.

"They took X rays. It didn't splinter, but it still hurts."

He opened the box and took out a gray gabardine topcoat. "You can drape this around you and they won't notice that you're dressed like a bum."

I looked down at my stained and wrinkled suit. "A little seedy," I agreed. "Who are we going to impress?"

"The oil crowd," he said. "I also bought one for myself."

"What about a razor?"

"I picked up an electric one."

"You think of everything."

"Somebody has to," he said.

After I shaved, I put on the topcoat, wearing it like a cape. Padillo had buttoned his up to the neck. Outside the hospital, we caught another cab and Padillo gave the driver the Bush Street address.

"What about Wanda?" I said.

"Wanda can take care of herself."

"Like a cat."

"That's right," he said. "Like a cat."

I wasn't old enough to remember it, but there had been a time when the oil company building on Bush Street had been the tallest in the city with its twenty-two stories. It had been built in 1923. Seven years later its principal rival built its own headquarters just down the street. It rose twenty-nine stories—out of spite, some said.

"What do you plan to do?" I said, as we got out of the cab in front of the twenty-nine-story building. "Wait till the last moment and then rise from the audience and say, 'Mr. Chairman, I think there is something you should know about the King of Llaquah'?"

"You'd like that, wouldn't you?"

"I always did have a keen sense of drama."

"Let's wait and see what happens," Padillo said.

"You think the king and Scales will really go through with it?"

"They'll try. Wouldn't you?"

"I don't know," I said.

The twenty-ninth floor was nicely paneled in oak and there was a rich carpet on the floor of the corridor which was peopled by half a dozen competent-looking men who wore dark suits and dubious expressions and who wanted to know who we were and why we thought we should be there.

"Your public relations man, Mr. Briggs, should have cleared us," Padillo said. One of the men who had questioned us ran his eyes down a list that he carried on a clipboard. He made a couple of checks with a pencil and nodded at the other man. "They're cleared," he said.

The other man pointed down the hall. "The third door, gentlemen."

"How'd you fix that?" I asked.

"I called Burmser and told him to arrange it."

"Did you tell him what had happened?"

Padillo shook his head. "I didn't get around to it for some reason."

The third door led into a large paneled conference room that was dominated by a huge, highly polished table that tapered at both ends and was surrounded by high-backed leather chairs. It was a table large enough to seat the nearly four dozen men who needed to be on hand when the time came to lay claim to nearly a third of the world's oil reserves.

Two 35mm cameras already had been set up, one on either side of the table, and their crews were fooling around with them. At one end of the room eight rows of chairs had been placed and they were almost filled with carefully made up, middle-aged women, nearly all of them wearing furs. Padillo and I found seats in the last row of chairs.

At precisely 10 A.M., a long line of men filed into the conference room, a little self-consciously, I thought, and took their seats at the table as the cameras recorded it all. A couple of still-photographers clicked away with their Canons and Nikons.

A few minutes later, the king and Scales came in, escorted by two distinguished-looking men whom I took to be the two companies' top executives. All took seats at the far end of the table. Someone had thought to furnish the king and Scales with new suits. The public relations man, I decided.

There was some preliminary murmuring as an aide passed out dark green folders to the men seated around the table. The king stared fixedly at the table top. Scales's hands fluttered nervously about, fingering his new tie and the buttons on his jacket. If someone had said boo, both of them would have jumped two feet.

The last person to enter the room was Wanda Gothar, wearing what seemed to be a mink stole. Underneath the stole was a dark gray suit that was smart enough to make the other women in the room appear dowdy. Wanda took a seat in the front row which seemed to have been reserved for her. She carried a large black envelope purse. From her seat she had a perfect view of the king and Scales at the far end of the table.

The king saw her first. His face collapsed as he clawed at Scale's shoulder, trying to get his attention. When Scales saw her he turned pale and became perfectly still. He looked sick. The chairman or president of one of the oil companies looked at him curiously and then leaned over and asked him something. Scales shook his head.

Wanda let them look at her for nearly a minute before she rose and started walking slowly toward the end of the long table where the two men sat, almost huddling against each other. She kept her right hand in the large black purse.

I thought I knew what was in that purse and started to rise, but Padillo caught my arm. "It's her deal now," he said. I sat back down.

Wanda stood near the end of the table, not more than two feet from Scales and the king who shrank back from her. The man who looked like a chairman of the board or at least president regarded her curiously and then turned away.

Her hand came slowly out of the purse. Her eyes were fixed on Scales and the king. Even from where I sat, I could see the terror that was smeared across their faces.

When her hand finally left her purse it didn't hold a gun, it held a piece of paper. She extended it to the king. I could see his hand tremble violently as he reached for it. He read the note and relief flooded his round face. He began to nod his bald head in eager, almost frantic agreement, handing the note to Scales who read it and began nodding, too. She stood there and watched them bob their heads for a long moment and then turned and walked out of the room.

"Let's go," Padillo said.

We caught up with Wanda about halfway down the carpeted corridor. Her face was pale and there was hard glitter in her eyes.

"You made it," she said, not seeming at all surprised. "Did Kragstein and Gitner?"

"No," Padillo said. "They're dead."

"Good. Aren't you going to interrupt the charade in there?"

"We were counting on you for that."

"I got what I wanted."

"They might bring it off," Padillo said.

She nodded. "I know. Why don't you stop them?"

"McCorkle would like to. He's got a speech all prepared."

She looked at me. "Well?"

"I've found that oil companies can take care of themselves without much help from me. I'm more interested in that note you handed the king."

"Yes," she said. "The note."

"How much cut did you ask for, Wanda?" Padillo said.

"No cut," she said, her tone as cold as her eyes.

"No?"

"No," she said. "I take it all. The entire five million."

"That'll buy Walter a lot of revenge."

She shook her head slowly. "You can't buy it for

the dead and there's something else about it you should learn."

"What?"

"The dead don't really care."

"Does five million dollars teach you that?"

She nodded. "It helps."

Chapter 26

They caught up with the king and Scales four days later in Milan, but not before they had withdrawn the five million dollars from the Swiss bank. When they were caught they had $52.56 in Italian lire between them. All they would say when asked about what had happened to the rest of the money was, "We spent it."

I read about it my first day back at work as I stood at the bar and drank a martini at eleven thirty in the morning because, for some reason, I thought it might stop my left arm from itching underneath the cast. It didn't, but it at least made it more bearable.

Padillo came in, took a letter from his pocket, and handed it to me. "It's to both of us," he said. The letter was from a Swiss bank and the most interesting paragraph read:

> Our client, Miss Wanda Gothar, has asked that we transfer the sum of $50,000 to a joint account which we have opened in your names at the Riggs National Bank in Washington, D.C. She also asked us to express her heartfelt appreciation for the courtesies that you extended to her during her recent holiday in America.

"Is it real?" I asked.

"I've already checked. It's real."

Karl moved down the bar toward us and started arranging some glasses. "Now that both of you guys are back—"

"He's got a lead on a Duesenberg," I told Padillo. "He wants us to lend him five thousand."

Padillo glanced at the letter that I still held. "Why not?" he said.

"All right," I said. "Buy it."

Karl beamed and then, because he wanted to demonstrate that he was really interested in his employers' welfare, he said, "How was San Francisco?"

"Fine," I said.

"You guys going to open another place out there?"

Padillo shook his head. "I don't think so."

"Why not?"

"We thought it lacked the proper ambience," I said.